Tom Slade's Double Dare

By

Percy Keese Fitzhugh

TOM SLADE'S DOUBLE DARE

CHAPTER I

THE LIGHT GOES OUT

If it were not for the very remarkable part played by the scouts in this strange business, perhaps it would have been just as well if the whole matter had been allowed to die when the newspaper excitement subsided. Singularly enough, that part of the curious drama which unfolded itself at Temple Camp is the very part which was never material for glaring headlines.

The main occurrence is familiar enough to the inhabitants of the neighborhood about the scout camp, but the sequel has never been told, for scouts do not seek notoriety, and the quiet woodland community in its sequestered hills is as remote from the turmoil and gossip of the world as if it were located at the North Pole.

But I know the story of Aaron Harlowe from beginning to end, and the part that Tom Slade played in it, and all the latter history of Goliath, as they called him. And I purpose to set all these matters down for your entertainment, for I think that first and last they make a pretty good camp-fire yarn.

For a week it had been raining at Temple Camp, and the ground was soggy from the continuous downpour. The thatched roofs of the more primitive type of cabins looked bedrabbled, like the hair of a bather emerging from the lake, and the more substantial shelters were crowded with the overflow from these and from tents deserted by troops and patrols that had been almost drowned out.

The grub boards out under the elm trees had been removed to the main pavilion. The diving springboard was submerged by the swollen lake, the rowboats rocked logily, half full of water, and the woods across the lake looked weird and dim through the incessant stream of rain, rain, rain.

The spring which supplied the camp and for years had been content to bubble in its modest abode among the rocks, burst forth from its shady and sequestered prison and came tumbling, roaring down out of the woods, like some boisterous marauder, and rushed headlong into the lake.

Being no respecter of persons, the invader swept straight through the cabin of the Silver Fox Patrol, and the Silver Fox Patrol took up their belongings and went over to the pavilion where they sat along the deep veranda with others, their chairs tilted back, watching the gloomy scene across the lake.

"This is good weather for the race," said Roy Blakeley.

"What race?" demanded Pee-wee Harris.

"The human race. No sooner said than stung. It's good weather to study monotony."

"All we can do is eat," said Pee-wee.

"Right the first time," Roy responded. "There's only one thing you don't like about meals and that's the time between them."

"What are we going to do for two hours, waiting for supper?" a scout asked.

"Search me," said Roy; "tell riddles, I guess. If we had some ham we'd have some ham and eggs, if we only had some eggs. We should worry. It's going to rain for forty-eight hours and three months more. That's what that scout from Walla-Walla told me."

"That's a dickens of a name for a city," said Westy Martin of Roy's patrol.

"It's a nice place, they liked it so much they named it twice," Roy said.

"There's a troop here all the way from Salt Lake," said Dorry Benton.

"They ought to have plenty of pep," said Roy.

"There's a troop came from Hoboken, too," Will Dawson observed.

"I don't blame them," Roy said. "There's a troop coming from Kingston next week. They've got an Eagle Scout, I understand."

"Don't you suppose I know that?" Pee-wee shouted. "Uncle Jeb had a letter from them yesterday; I saw it."

"Was it in their own handwriting?"

"What do you mean?" Pee-wee demanded disgustedly. "How can a troop have a handwriting?"

"They must be very ignorant," Roy said. "Can you send an animal by mail?"

"Sure you can't!" Pee-wee shouted.

"That's where you're wrong," said Roy. "I got a letter with a seal on it."

"Can you unscramble eggs?" Pee-wee demanded.

"There you go, talking about eats again. Can't you wait two hours?"

There was nothing to do but wait, and watch the drops as they pattered down on the lake.

"This is the longest rain in history except the reign of Queen Elizabeth," Roy said. "If I ever meet Saint Swithin — — "

This sort of talk was a sample of life at Temple Camp for seven days past. Those who were not given to jollying and banter had fallen back on checkers and dominos and other wild sports. A few of the more adventurous and reckless made birchbark ornaments, while those who were in utter despair for something to do wrote letters home.

Several dauntless spirits had braved the rain to catch some fish, but the fish, themselves disgusted, stayed down at the bottom of the lake, out of the wet, as Roy said. It was so wet that even the turtles wouldn't come out without umbrellas.

Rain, rain, rain. It flowed off the pavilion roof like a waterfall. It shrunk tent canvas which pulled on the ropes and lifted the pegs out of the soggy ground. It buried the roads in mud. Hour in and hour out the scouts sat along the back of the deep veranda, beguiling their enforced leisure with banter and riddles and camp gossip.

On Friday afternoon a brisk wind arose and blew the rain sideways so that most of the scouts withdrew from their last entrenchment and went inside. You have to take off your hat to a rain which can drive a scout in out of the open.

It began blowing in across the veranda in fitful little gusts and within an hour the wind had lashed itself into a gale. A few of the hardier spirits, including Roy, held their ground on the veranda, squeezing back against the shingled side whenever an unusually severe gust assailed them.

There is no such thing as twilight in such weather, but the sodden sky grew darker, and the mountainside across the lake became gloomier and more forbidding as the night drew on apace.

The few remaining stragglers on the veranda watched this darkening scene with a kind of idle half interest, ducking the occasional gusts.

"How would you like to be out on the lake now?" one asked.

The question directed their gaze out upon the churning, black sheet of water before them. The lake, lying amid those frowning, wooded hills, was somber enough at all times, and a quiet gloom pervaded it which imparted a rare charm. But now, in the grip of the rain and wind, the enshrouding night made the lake seem like a place haunted, and the enclosing mountains desolate and forlorn.

"I'll swim across with anybody," said Hervey Willetts.

He belonged in a troop from western New York and reveled in stunts which bespoke a kind of blithe daring. No one took him up and silence reigned for a few minutes more.

"There's the little light on the top of the mountain," said Will Dawson of Roy's patrol. "If there's anybody up there, I hope he has an umbrella."

But of course there was no one up there. For weeks the tiny light away up on the summit of that mountain wilderness had puzzled the scouts of camp. They had not, indeed, been able to determine that it was a light; it seemed rather a tiny patch of brightness which was always brighter when the moon shone. This had led to the belief that it was caused by some kind of natural phenomena.

The scouts fixed their gaze upon it, watching it curiously for a few moments.

"It isn't a reflection, that's sure," said Roy, "or we wouldn't see it on a night like this."

"It's a phosphate," said Pee-wee.

"It's a chocolate soda," said Roy.

"You're crazy!" Pee-wee vociferated. "Phosphate is something that shines in the dark."

"You mean phosphorus," said Westy Martin.

That seemed a not unlikely explanation. But the consensus of opinion in camp was that the bright patch was the reflection of some powerful light in the low country on the opposite side of the mountain.

"It's a mystery," said Pee-wee, "that's what it is."

Suddenly, while they gazed, it went out. They watched but it did not come again. And the frowning, jungle-covered, storm beaten summit was enshrouded again in ghostly darkness. And the increasing gale beat the lake, and the driven rain assailed the few stragglers on the veranda with lashing fury. And across the black water, in that ghoul-haunted, trackless wilderness, could be heard the sound of timber being rent in splinters and of great trees crashing down the mountainside.

Suddenly a word from Westy Martin aroused them all like a cannon shot.

"Look!" he shouted, "Look! Look at the springboard!"

Every one of them looked, speechless, astonished, aghast, at the sight which they beheld before their very eyes.

CHAPTER II

THE BRIDGE

There, just below them was the springboard an inch or two above the surface of the lake. Ordinarily it projected from the shore nearly a yard above the water, but lately the swollen lake had risen above it. Now, however, it was visible again just above the surface.

This meant that the water had receded more in an hour than it had risen in a whole week. The strong wind was blowing toward the pavilion and would naturally force the water up along that shore. But in spite of the wind the water in the lake was receding at an alarming rate. Something was wrong. The little trickle from the spring up behind the camp had grown into a torrent and was pouring into the lake. Yet the water in the lake was receding.

Down out of the mountain wilderness across the water came weird noises, caused no doubt by the tumult of the wind in the intricate fastnesses and by the falling of great trees, but the sounds struck upon the ears of the besieged listeners like voices wild and unearthly. The banging of the big shutters of the pavilion was heard in echo as the furious gale bore the sounds back from the mountain and the familiar, homely noise was conjured into a kind of ghostly clamor.

"There goes Pee-wee's signal tower," a scout remarked, and just as he spoke, the little rustic edifice which had been the handiwork and pride of the tenderfoots went crashing to the ground while out of the woods across the water came sounds as of merry laughter at its downfall.

"Something's wrong over on the other side," said Westy Martin of Roy's patrol; "the lake's breaking through over there."

Scarcely had he uttered the words when all the scouts of the little group were at the railing craning their necks and straining their eyes trying to see across the water. But the wind and rain beat in their faces and the driving downpour formed an impenetrable mist.

As they withdrew again into the comparative shelter of the porch they saw a young fellow standing with his bare arm upraised against the door-jam, watching and listening. This was the young camp assistant, Tom Slade. He had evidently come out to fasten the noisy shutters and had paused to contemplate the tempest.

"Some storm, hey, Tomasso?" said Roy.

"I think the water's going out through the cove," said Tom. "It must have washed away the land over there."

"Let it go, we can't stop it," said Roy.

"If it's running out into the valley, it's good-night to Berry's garage, and the bridge too," said Tom.

The young assistant was popular with the boys at camp, and struck by this suggestion of imminent catastrophe, they clustered about him, listening eagerly. So loud was the noise of the storm, so deafening the sound of rending timber on that gale-swept height before them, that Tom had to raise his voice to make himself heard. The danger to human life which he had been the first to think of, gave the storm new terror to these young watchers. It needed only this touch of mortal peril in that panorama of dreadfulness to arouse them, good scouts that they were, to the chances of adventure and the possibility of service.

"We can't do anything, can we?" one asked. "It's too late now, isn't it?"

"It's either too late or it isn't," said Tom Slade; "and it's for us to see. I was thinking of Berry's place, and I was thinking of the crowd that's coming up tonight on the bus. If the water has broken through across the lake and is pouring into the valley, it'll wash away the bridge. The bus ought to be here now. There are two troops from the four-twenty train at Catskill. Maybe the train is late on account of the weather. If the bridge is down...."

"Call up Berry's place and find out," said Westy Martin.

"That's just what has me worrying," said Tom; "Berry's doesn't answer."

CHAPTER III

AN IMPORTANT MISSION

Temple Camp was situated on a gentle slope close to the east shore of the lake. Save for this small area of habitable land the lake was entirely surrounded by mountains. And it was the inverted forms of these mountains reflected in the water which gave it the somber hue whence the lake derived its name. On sunless days and in the twilight, the water seemed as black as night.

Directly across the water from the camp, the most forbidding of those surrounding heights reared its deeply wooded summit three thousand feet above the sea level. A wilderness of tangled underbrush, like barbed wire entanglements, baffled the hardiest adventurer. No scout had penetrated those dismal fastnesses which the legend of camp reputed to be haunted.

Beside the rocky base of this mountain was a tiny cove, a dim, romantic little place, where the water was as still as in a pool. Its two sides were the lower reaches of the great mountain and its neighbor, and all that prevented the cove from being an outlet was a little hubble of land which separated this secluded nook from a narrow valley, or gully, beyond.

Sometimes, indeed, after a rainy spell the water in the cove overflowed this little hubble of land enough to trickle through into the gully, and then you could pick fish up with your hands where they flopped about marooned in the channel below. Probably this gully was an old dried-up stream bed.

About a mile from the lake it became wider and was intersected by a road. Here it was that the bridge spanned the hollow. And here it was, right in the hollow near the bridge, that Ebon Berry had his rural garage. Along this road the old bus lumbered daily, bringing new arrivals to camp and touching at villages beyond.

If, indeed, the swollen lake had washed away the inner shore of the cove, the sequel would be serious if not tragic at that quiet road crossing. The question was, had this happened, and if so, had the bus reached the fatal spot? All that the boys knew was that the bus was long overdue and that Berry's "did not answer." And that the fury of the storm was rising with every minute.

Tom Slade spoke calmly as was his wont. No storm could arouse him out of his stolid, thoughtful habit.

"A couple of scoutmasters have started along the road," he said, "to see what they can find out. How about you, Hervey? Are you game to skirt the lake? How about you, Roy? There may be danger over there."

"Believe me, I hope it'll wait till we get there," said Hervey Willetts.

"I'll go!" shouted Pee-wee.

"You'll go—in and get supper," said Tom. "I want just three fellows; I'm not going to overload a boat in this kind of weather. I'll take Roy and Hervey and Westy, if you fellows are game to go. You go in and get a lantern, Pee-wee."

"And don't forget to leave some pie for those two troops that are coming on the bus," added Roy.

Pee-wee did better than bring a lantern; he brought also three oilskin jackets and hats which the younger boys donned. He must also have advertised the adventurous expedition during his errand indoors, for a couple of dozen envious scouts followed him out and watched the little party depart.

The four made their way against a blown rain which all but blinded them and streamed from their hats and rendered their storm jackets quite useless. Tom wore khaki trousers and a pongee shirt which clung to him like wet tissue paper. If one cannot be thoroughly dry the next best thing is to be thoroughly wet.

They chose the widest and heaviest of the boats, a stout old tub with two pairs of oarlocks. Each of the four manned an oar and pulled with both hands. It was almost impossible to get started against the wind, and when at last their steady, even pulling overcame the deterring power of the gale they were able to move at but a snail's pace. They followed the shoreline, keeping as close in as they could, preferring the circuitous route to the more perilous row across the lake.

As their roundabout voyage brought them to the opposite shore, their progress became easier, for the mountain rising sheer above them protected them from the wind.

"Let her drift a minute," said Tom, panting; "lift your oars."

It was the first word that any of them had spoken, so intense had been their exertions.

"She's going straight ahead," said Westy.

"What's that?" said Roy suddenly. "Look out!"

He spoke just in time to enable them to get out of the path of a floating tree which was drifting rapidly in the same direction as the boat. Its great mass of muddy roots brushed against them.

"It's just as I thought," Tom said; "the water must be pouring out through the cove. We're caught in it. Let's try to get a little off shore; we'll have one of those trees come tumbling down on our heads the first thing we know."

"Not so easy," said Hervey, as they tried to backwater and at the same time get out from under the mountain.

"Put her in reverse," said Roy, who never failed to get the funny squint on a situation.

But there was no use, the rushing water had them in its grip and they were borne along pell-mell, with trees and broken limbs which had fallen down the mountainside.

They were directly opposite the camp now, and cheerful lights could be seen in the pavilion where the whole camp community was congregated, safe from the storm. The noises which had seemed weird enough at camp were appalling now, as out of that havoc far above them, great bowlders came tumbling down into the lake with loud splashes.

Tom realized, all too late, the cause of the dreadful peril they were in. Out on the body of the lake and toward the camp shore the wind was blowing a gale from the mountains and, as it were, forcing the water back. But directly under the mountain there was no wind, and their position was as that of a person who is under the curve of a waterfall. And here, because there was no wind to counteract it, the water was rushing toward what was left of the cove. It was like a rapid river flowing close to the shore and bearing upon its hurrying water the débris which had crashed down from that lonesome, storm-torn height.

The boat was caught in this rushing water and the danger was increased by its closeness to the shore where every missile of rock or tree, cast by that frowning monster, might at any minute dash the craft to splinters.

The little flickering lights which shone through the spray and fine blown rain across that black water seemed very cheerful and inviting now.

CHAPTER IV

THE TREE

"We're in a bad fix," said Tom; "let's try to make a landing and see if we can scramble along shore to the cove."

It is doubtful whether they could have scrambled along that precipitous bank, but in any case, so great was the impetus of the rushing water that even making a landing was impossible. The boat was borne along with a force that all their exertions could not counteract, headlong for the cove.

"What can we do?" Roy asked.

"The only thing that I know of," said Tom, "is to get within reach of the shore in the cove. If we can do that we might get to safety even if we have to jump."

Presently the boat went careening into the cove; an appalling sound of scraping, then of tearing, was heard beneath it, it reared up forward, spilling its occupants into the whirling water and, settling sideways, remained stationary.

The boys found themselves clinging to the branches of a broken tree which was wedged crossways in the cove, its trunk entirely submerged. It formed a sort of makeshift dam and the boat, caught in its branches, added to the obstruction.

If it had not been for this tree the boat would have been borne upon the flood, with what tragic sequel who shall say?

"All right," said Tom, "we're lucky; keep hold of the branches, it's only a few feet to shore; careful how you step. If you let go it's all over. We could never swim in this torrent."

"Where do you suppose this tree came from?" Roy asked.

"From the top of the mountain for all I know," Tom answered. "Watch your step and follow me. We're in luck."

"You don't call this luck, do you?" Westy asked.

"Watch me, I can go scout-pace on the trunk," said Hervey, handing himself along.

"Never mind any of those stunts," said Tom; "you watch what you're doing and follow me."

"The pleasure is mine," said Hervey; "a scout is always — whoa! There's where I nearly dipped the dip. Watch me swing over this branch. I bet you can't hang by your knees — like this."

There are some people who think that trees were made to bear fruit and to afford shade, and to supply timber. But that is a mistake; they were made for Hervey Willetts. They were the scenes of his gayest stunts. He had even been known to dive under the water and shimmy up a tree that was reflected there. He even claimed that he got a splinter in his hand, so doing! Upside down or wedged across a channel under water, trees were all the same to Hervey Willetts. He lived in trees. He knew nothing whatever about the different kinds of trees and he could not tell spruce from walnut. But he could hang by one leg from a rotten branch, the while playing a harmonica. He was for the boy scout movement, because he was for movement generally. As long as the scouts kept moving, he was with them. He had a lot of merit badges but he did not know how many. "He should worry," as Roy said of him.

"Here's a good one — known as the jazzy-jump," he exclaimed. "Put your left foot...."

"You put your left foot on the trunk and don't let go the branches and follow me," said Tom, soberly. "Do you think this is a picnic we're on?"

"After you, my dear Tomasso," said Hervey, blithely. "I guess we're not going to be killed after all, hey?"

"I'm afraid not," said Tom.

"I wish I had an ice cream soda, I know that," said Roy.

"Careful how you step ashore now," Tom said.

"Terra cotta at last," said Roy; "I mean terra firma."

"Jump it," called Hervey, who was behind Roy.

Thus, emerging from a peril, which none but Tom had fully realized, they found themselves on the comparatively low shore of the cove. The tree, itself a victim of the storm, poked its branches up out of the black water like specters, which seemed the more grewsome as they swayed in the wind. These had guided the little party to shore.

So it was that that once stately denizen of the lofty forest had paused here to make a last stand against the storm which had uprooted it. So it was that this fallen monarch, friend of the scouts, had contrived to check somewhat the mad rush of water out of their beloved lake, and had guided four of them to safety.

CHAPTER V
WIN OR LOSE

The dying mission of that noble tree suggested a thought to Tom. The water from the lake was pouring over it, though checked somewhat by the tree and the boat. If this tree, firmly wedged in place, could be made the nucleus of a mass of wreckage, the flood might be effectually checked, temporarily, at least. One thing, a moment's glance at the condition of the cove showed all too certainly what must have happened at the road-crossing. That the little rustic bridge there could have withstood the first overwhelming rush of the flood was quite unthinkable. Berry's garage too, perched on the edge of the hollow, must have been swept away.

THE TREE POKED ITS BRANCHES UP OUT OF THE BLACK WATER AND GUIDED THEM TO SAFETY.

Tom Slade's Double Dare.   Page 25

And where was the lumbering old bus? That was the question now. If it had been a motor bus its lights might have foretold the danger. But it was one of those old-fashioned horse-drawn stages which are still seen in mountain districts.

In all that tumult of storm, Tom Slade paused to think. All about them was Bedlam. Down the precipitous mountainside hard by, were crashing the torn and uprooted trophies of the storm high in those dizzy recesses above, where eagles, undisturbed by any human presence, made their homes upon the crags. The rending and crashing up there was conjured by the distance into a hundred weird and uncanny voices which now and again seemed like the wailing of human souls.

The rush of water, gathering force in the narrow confines of the cove, became a torrent and threw a white spray in the faces of the boys as it beat against the fallen tree. It seemed strange that they could be so close to this paroxysm of the elements, in the very center of it as one might say, and yet be safe. Nature was in a mad turmoil all about them, yet by a lucky chance they stood upon a little oasis of temporary refuge.

"There are two things that have to be done—quick," said Tom. "Somebody has got to pick his way down the west shore back to camp. It's through the mountains and maybe two of you had better go. Here, take my compass," he added, handing it to Westy. "Have you got some matches?"

"I've got my flashlight," said Roy.

So it fell out that Westy and Roy were the ones to make the journey back to camp.

"Keep as close to the shore as you can, it's easier going and shorter," Tom said. "Anyway, use the compass and keep going straight south till you see the lights at camp, then turn east. You ought to be able to do it in an hour. Tell everybody to get busy and throw everything in the water that'll help plug up the passage. Chuck in the logs from the woodshed."

"How about the remains of Pee-wee's signal tower?"

"Good, chuck that in. Throw in everything that can be spared. Most of it will drift over here and get caught in the rush. If the wind dies it will all come over. Hurry up! I'll stay here and try to get in place anything more that comes in in the meantime. There are a lot of broken limbs and things around here. Hurry up now, beat it! And don't stop till you get there.... Don't let anybody try to start over in a boat," he called after them.

Scarcely had they set off when he turned to Hervey Willetts, placing both his hands on the boy's shoulders. The rain was streaming down from Hervey's streaked hair. The funny little rimless hat cut full of holes which he wore on the side of his head and which was the pride of his life had collapsed by reason of being utterly soaked, for he had very early discarded the oilskin "roof" in preference for this old love. One of his stockings was falling down and he hoisted this up as Tom spoke to him.

"Hervey, I'm glad you're going alone, because you won't have to do any stunts for anybody's benefit. You're going to keep your mind on just one thing. Understand?"

"I can think of nine things at once," said Hervey, blithely, "and sing Over There and eat a banana at the same time. How's that?"

"That's fine. Now listen—just two seconds. You're to hit right straight up through this country—north. You notice I gave the compass to Roy? That's because I know you can't get rattled when you're alone and when you put your mind on a thing. You're to go straight north till you reach the road. I'll have to keep the lantern here, but you won't need it. You've got about a quarter of a mile of rough country and then easy going. Straight north beyond the road is Crows Nest Mountain. Turn around, that's right. Shut your eyes. One—two—three—four—five. Now open them suddenly. You see that black bulk. That's Crows Nest. Now you know how to see a dark thing in the dark...."

"Do you know how to tell time with a clothespin?"

"Never mind that. About every ten minutes stop and shut your eyes and old Crows Nest will guide you. Don't get rattled. When you get to the road wait for the bus and stop it. If it has passed by now, we can't help it. I'm afraid it has. But if it hasn't, there are two troops in it and their lives depend on you. Now get out of here—quick!"

"What was that?" Hervey said, pausing and clutching Tom's arm.

"What was what?"

"That sound—away off. Hear it?"

Amid the wild clamor of the tempest, the dashing of the impeded water close by, and the ghostly voices up in that mountain wilderness, there sounded, far off, subdued and steady, a low melodious call, spent and thin from the distance, and blended with the myriad sounds of the raging storm.

"It's the train," said Tom.

Still Hervey did not move, only clutched his companion's arm. One second—two seconds—three, four, five, six. The sound died away in the uproar of wind and rain.... Still the two paused for just a moment more, as if held by a spell.

"A mile and a half—four miles," said Tom. "Four miles of road. A mile and a half of hills and swamps. They're at the station now. You can't do it, kid. But you'd better fail trying than not try at all. What do you say?"

There was no answer, for Hervey Willetts had already plunged into the torrent, by which hazardous act ten minutes might be saved. Or everything lost. Tom caught a glimpse of that funny perforated hat bobbing in the rushing water of the cove, pulled tight down over its young owner's ears. Sober as his thoughts were in the face of harrowing peril, he could not repress a smile that Hervey should toss his life so blithely into the enterprise and yet be careful to save that precious hat. He was more proud of it than of all his deeds of reckless valor.

Tom knew there was no restraining him, or advising him. He knew no more of discipline than a skylark does. He was either the best scout in the world or no scout at all, as you choose to look at it. He was going upon this business in reckless haste, without forethought or caution. He would stake his life to save twenty yards of distance. There was no discretion in his valor. Blithe young gambler that he was, he would do the thing in his own way. No one could tell him. Tom knew the utter futility of shouting any last warnings or instructions to him.

For Hervey Willetts was like a shot out of a rifle. With him it was a case of hit or miss. He had no rules....

CHAPTER VI

SHADOWS OF THE NIGHT

One thing Hervey did bear in mind, and that was what Tom had told him about how to distinguish a dark object in the dark. He would not remember this twenty-four hours hence, but he remembered it then, and that is saying much for him. He tried to improve upon the formula by experimenting with his eyes cross-eyed, but it didn't work. Skirting the lower western reach of the mountain and beyond, in the comparatively flat country, he kept squinting away at old Crows Nest and its shadowy, black mass guided him. "Slady's got the right dope on mountains," he said to himself.

The race was about as Tom had said; four miles for the horses, against a mile and a half for Hervey. Both routes were bad, Hervey's the worse of the two. All things considered, hills, muddy roads, trackless woodland, swampy areas, it should take the heavily loaded team a little over an hour to reach the bridge. By Tom's calculation it must take Hervey at least an hour and a half.

So there you are.

Going straight north, Hervey would have that dim black mass, hovering on the verge of invisibility, to guide him. Traveling a little west of north he might have reached the road at a nearer point. But here the traveling was bad and the danger of getting lost greater. Tom had weighed one thing against another and told Hervey to go straight north.

Hervey found the first half hour of his journey very difficult, picking his way around the base of the mountain. Beyond the country was flat and comparatively open, being mostly sparse woodland. The wind was very keen here, since there was no mountain to break its force and the rain blew in his face, almost blinding him.

Again and again he wiped his dripping face with his sleeve and plodded on, picking out his beacon now and again in the darkness. It was surprising how easy it was for him to do this by the little trick of which Tom had told him. His eyes would just catch the mountain for a second, then it would evaporate in the surrounding blackness, like breath on a pane of glass.

Suddenly, something happened which quite unnerved him. He was hurrying through a patch of woodland when, not more than ten feet ahead of him, he was certain that he saw something dark glide from one tree to another.

He stopped short, his heart in his mouth. The minutes, he knew, were precious, but he could not move. The wind in the trees moaned like some lost soul, and in his stark fear the beating of the drops on the leafy carpet startled him. He heard these because he was standing still, and the ceasing of his own footfalls emphasized the steady patter. Somewhere, in all that stormy solitude and desolation, an uncanny owl hooted its dismal song.

Hervey did not move.

It was not till he bethought him of those horses lumbering along the road ever nearer and nearer to that trap of death that he got control of himself and started off.

It was just the gloom of those dark woods, the play of some freakish and deceptive shadow conjuring itself into a human presence, that he had seen.... Who would be out in that lonely wood on such a night?

With a sudden, desperate impulse to challenge his fear and have done with it, he stepped briskly toward the tree to glance about it and dispel his illusion. If it was just some branch broken by the wind and hanging loose....

He approached the trunk and edged around it. As he did so a form moved around the trunk also. Hervey paused. The pounding of his heart seemed louder than the noises of the storm. In his throat was a queer burning sensation. He could not speak. He could not stir. The dark form moved again, ever so little....

CHAPTER VII

THE LIGHT THAT FAILED

The suspense was worse than any outcome could be, and Hervey, in another impulse of desperation, took a step to the right, then quickly another to the left. This ruse brought the two face to face. And in a flash Hervey realized that he had little to fear from one who had tried so desperately to escape his notice.

The figure was that of a young man, his raiment torn and disordered and utterly drenched. He wore a plaid cap, which being pulled down over his ears by reason of the wind, gave him an appearance of toughness which his first words belied.

"You needn't be afraid," he said.

"I'm not afraid," said Hervey. "Who are you?"

"Did you hear some one scream?" the stranger asked.

"Scream? No. It was the wind, I guess. Are you lost, or what?"

"I want to get out of here, that's all," the young man said. "This place is full of children screaming. Did you ever kill anybody?"

"No," said Hervey, somewhat agitated.

The stranger placed a trembling hand on Hervey's shoulder. "Do you know a person can scream after he's dead?" he said.

"I don't know," said Hervey, somewhat alarmed and not knowing what to say. "Anyway, I have to hurry; it's up to me to save some people's lives. There's a bridge washed away along the road."

He did not wait longer to talk with this singular stranger, but thoughts of the encounter lingered in his mind, particularly the young fellow's speech about dead people and children screaming. As he hurried on, Hervey concluded that the stranger was demented and had probably wandered away from some village in the neighborhood. He had reason later to recall this encounter, but he soon forgot it in the more urgent matter of reaching the road.

He had now about half a mile of level country to traverse, consisting of fields separated by stone walls. The land was soggy, and here and there in the lower places were areas of water. These he would not take the time to go around, but plunged through them, often going knee deep into the marshy bottom. It was sometimes with difficulty that he was able to extricate his leg from these soggy entanglements.

But he no longer needed the uncertain outline of that black mass amid the surrounding blackness to guide him, for now the cheerful lights of an isolated house upon the road shone in the distance. There was the road, sure enough, though he could not see it.

"That's what Slady calls deduction," he panted, as he trudged on, running when he could, and dragging his heavy, mud-bedraggled feet out of the mire every dozen steps or so. Over a stone wall he went and scrambled to his feet and hastened on.

The lights in the house cheered and guided him and he made straight for this indubitable beacon. "Mountains are all—all right," he panted, "but kerosene lamps—for—for—mine. I hope that—bunch—doesn't go to—bed." His heart was pounding and he had a cruel stitch in his side from running, which pained him excruciatingly when he ran fast. He tried scout pace but it didn't work; he was not much of a hand for that kind of thing. "It's—it's—all—right when—you're running through—the—handbook," he said, "but—but...."

Over another stone wall he went, tearing a great gash in his trousers, exposing the limb to rain and wind. The ground was better for a space and he ran desperately. Every breath he drew pained him, now and again he staggered slightly, but he kept his feet and plunged frantically on.

Then one of the lights in the house went out. Then another. There was only one now. "That's—that's—what—it means for—for—people to—to go to—

to bed early," he panted with difficulty. "I—I always—said——" He had not the breath to finish, but it is undoubtedly true that he had always been a staunch advocate of remaining up all night.

He fixed his eyes upon the one remaining light and ran with utter desperation. His breathing was spasmodic, he reeled, pulled himself together by sheer will, and stumbled on. On the next stone wall he made a momentary concession to his exhaustion and paused just a moment, holding his aching side.

Then he was off again, running like mad. The single little light seemed twinkling and hazy and he brushed his streaming face with his sleeve so that he might see it the more clearly. But it looked dull, more like a little patch of brightness than a shining light. Either it was failing, or he was.

He had to hold his stinging side and gulp for every breath he drew, but he ran with all his might and main. He was too spent and dizzy to keep his direction without that distant light, and he knew it. He was not Tom Slade to be sure of himself in complete darkness. He was giddy—on the verge of collapse. The bee-line of his course loosened and became erratic. But if his legs were weakening his will was strong, and he staggered, reeled, ran.

On, on, on, he sped, falling forward now, rather than running, but keeping his feet by the sheer power of his will. His heart seemed up in his mouth and choking him. With one hand he grasped the flying shred of his torn trousers and tried to wipe the blood from the cut in his leg. Thus for just a second his progress was impeded.

That was the last straw. The trifling movement lost him his balance, his exhausted and convulsed body went round like a top and he lay breathing in little jerks on the swampy ground.

One second. Two seconds. Three seconds. In another five seconds he would rise. He raised himself on one trembling arm and looked about. He brushed his soaking hair back from his eyes and looked again.

"Where—what—where—is—it—anyway?" he panted. He did not know which direction was north or south or east or west. He only knew that a dagger was sticking in his side and that he could not rise....

Yes, he could. He pulled himself together, rested a moment on his knees, staggered to his feet and looked around.

"Where—where—th—the dickens—is north?"

He turned and looked around. He looked around the other way. Nothing but desolation and darkness. He thought of what Tom had told him and, closing his eyes, opened them suddenly. The mountain must have been too near to show in outline now; it had probably melted into the general landscape. There was just an even, solid blackness all about him. The wind moaned, and somewhere, high and far off, he heard the screech of an eagle. But at least the rain did not assail him as it had done. This, however, was small comfort. He had lost, failed, and he knew it.

In pitiable despair, in the anguish of defeat, he looked about him again in every direction, as if to beseech the angry night to give him back his one little beacon, and let him only save those people if he died for it.

But there was no light anywhere. It had gone out.

CHAPTER VIII

ALMOST

Well, he would not go back. They should find him right there, his body marking the very last foot he had been able to go. He would die as those brother scouts of his would have to die. He would not go back.

That good rule of the scouts to stop and think was not in Hervey's line. But he would do the next best thing—a thing very characteristic of Hervey Willetts. He would take a chance and start running. Yes, that would be better. There would be just one chance in four of his going in the right direction. But he had taken bigger chances than that before. Anyway, the rain was ceasing. And he soon overcame the sentimental notion of just lying there.

The momentary rest had restored some measure of his strength. The aching in his side was not so acute. The land was not so muddy where he was and he took off his jacket and washed some of the heavy mud from his shoes.

Then he started off pell-mell. Who shall say what good angel prompted him to look behind? Perhaps it was the little god Billikins of whom you are to know more in these pages. But look behind Hervey Willetts did. And there in the distance, very tiny but very clear, was a spark bobbing in the darkness.

He paused and watched it over his shoulder. It moved along slowly, very slowly. It disappeared. Then appeared again. And now it moved a little faster. A little faster still. Now it moved along at an even, steady rate. The long, hard pull up Cheery Hill was over, and the horses were jogging along the road. Oh, how well Hervey knew that lantern which hung under the rear step of the clumsy, lumbering old bus.

Then it had not passed.

Hervey Willetts was himself now. Tearing a loose shred from his tattered trousers, he soaked it in a little puddle, then stuffed it in his mouth. He clasped his jack-knife in one fist and a twig in the other. He drew up his belt. He took that precious hat off and stuffed it in his pocket, campaign buttons and all. Ah, no, he did not throw it away. He ripped off another rag and tied it fast around his neck and he bound his scarf around his forehead. He knew all these little tricks of the runner. It was not thought, but action now.

But, oh, Hervey, Hervey! What sort of a scout are you? Did you not know that the shriek of the eagle must have been from the mountain in the north? Did you not know that eagles live on mountain crags? Why did you not face into the wind and you would have headed north? When the rain did not blow in your face or against either cheek, that was because you were facing south. It had not stopped raining. It was raining and blowing foryour sake and you did not know it. You were hunting for a kerosene lamp!

But there are scouts and scouts.

Bareheaded, half naked, he sped through the darkness like a ghostly specter of the night. He headed for a point some fifty yards ahead of the bus. He knew that coming from behind he could not catch it in time. He was running to intercept it, not to overtake it. He was running at right angles to it and for a point ahead of it. Therein lay his only chance, and not a very good chance. By all the rules there was no chance. By the divine law which gives power to desperation, there was — a little.

He ran in utter abandonment, in frenzy. Some power outside of himself bore him on. What else? Like a fiend, with arms swinging and head swathed in a crazy rag, he moved through wind and storm, invincible, indomitable! His head throbbed, his mouth was thick, his side ached, but he seemed beyond the power of these things now. Over the fences he went, leaving shreds of clothing blowing in the gale, and tearing his flesh on stone walls. In the madness of despair, and in the insane resolve that despair begets, he sped on, on, on....

The bus was now almost even with his course. He changed his course to keep ahead of it. The lumbering old rattle-trap gave out a human note now, which cheered the runner. He could hear the voices within it. Very faint, but still he could hear them. He knew he could not make himself heard because the wind was the other way. Besides which, he had not the voice to call. His whole frame was trembling; he could not have spoken even.

On, on, on. The trees passed him like trees seen from a train window. He turned the wet rag in his mouth to draw a little more moisture from it. He clutched his sweating hands tighter around the knife and twig. He shook the blowing, dripping hair from his eyes. Forward, forward! If he slackened his speed now he would fall—collapse. Like a top, his speed kept him up.

Running straight ahead he would about run into the bus, which meant that it was gaining on him. Again he bent his course to a point ahead of it. Each maneuver of this kind narrowed the angle between himself and the bus until soon he would be pursuing it. The angle would be no more. He would be running after the bus and losing ground.

By a supreme, final spurt, he had now a fair chance to make the road and intercept the bus before it reached the broad, level stretch to the bridge. Should it reach that point his last chance would have vanished.

In this desperate pass he tried to shout, but found, as the spent runner usually does, that he was almost voiceless. A feeble call was all he could manage, and on the contrary wind and noise of the storm, this was quite inadequate. He could only stumble on, borne up by his indomitable will. He was weakening and he knew it.

Yet the light of the bus so near him gave him fresh hope, and with it fresh strength. It seemed a kind of perversity of fate that he should have reached a point ordinarily within earshot, and yet could not make his approach known.

Just as the bus was passing his course, and when it was perhaps three or four hundred feet distant, Hervey, putting all his strength into a final spurt, sped forward in a blind frenzy like one possessed. He saw the bus go by;

heard the voices within it. Throwing his jack-knife from him in a kind of frantic, maniacal desperation, he tried to scream, and finding that he could not, that his voice was dead while yet his limbs lived, and that his panting throat was clogged up and his nerves jangled and uncontrollable, he bounded forward in a kind of delirium of concentrated effort.

Then, suddenly, his foot sank into a hole. Perhaps with a little calmness and patience he could have released it. But in his wild hurry he tried to wrench it out. A sudden, sharp pain rewarded this insane effort. He lost his balance and went sprawling to the ground, another quick, excruciating twinge accompanying his fall, and lay there on the soggy ground like a woodchuck in a trap.

The old bus went lumbering by.

CHAPTER IX

THE HERO

The best account of this business was given by Darby Curren, the bus driver, or Curry, as the boys called him.

"We was jes' comin' onter the good road, we was, and I was jes' about goin' ter give Lefty a taste o' the whip ter let 'er know ter wake up. Them kids inside was a hollerin', 'Hit 'er up!" 'Step on 'er!' 'Give 'er the gas!' and all sech nonsense. Well, by gorry, I never seed sech a night since Noah sailed away in the ark, I didn't. So ye'll understand I was'n' fer bein' surprised at nuthin' I see. Ghosts nor nuthin'.

"Well, all of a sudden Lefty begins to jump and rear step sideways and was like to drag us all in the ditch when what do I see but that there thing, like a ghost or somethin' it was, hangin' onter her bridle. It was makin' some kind of a noise, I dunno what. First off I thought plum certain it was a ghost. Then I thought it was Hasbrooks' boy, that's what I thought, on account o' him havin' them fits and maybe bein' buried alive. It was me that druv the hearse fer 'im only a week back. And I says then to Corby that was sittin' with me, I says, no son o' mine that ever had them fits would be buried in three days, not if I knowed it. Safety first, I said, dead or livin'.

"Well, I hollered to him what he wanted there and I didn't get no answer so I got down. And all the rest o' that howlin' pack got out, and the two men. I guess they thought we was held up, Jesse James like. Only the little codger stayed inside.

"Well, there he was, all tore and bloody and not enough duds left to stop up a rat-hole. And we hed ter force his hand open, he was hangin' onter the bridle that hard."

Well, that was about all there was to it; the rest was told by many mouths. They forced open his grip on the horse's bridle and he collapsed and lay unconscious on the ground. They lifted him and carried him gently into the bus, and laid him on one of the long seats. His left foot was shoeless and lacerated.

There were a couple of first aid scouts in the party, and they did what they could for him, bathing his face and trying to restore some measure of repose to his jangled nerves. They washed his torn foot with antiseptic while one kept a cautious hold upon his fluttering pulse. They administered a heart stimulant out of their kit, and waited. He did not speak nor open his eyes, save momentarily at intervals, when he stared vacantly. But the stout heart which had served him in his superhuman effort, would not desert him now, and in a little while the brother scout who held his wrist laid it gently down and, in a kind of freakish impulse, made the full scout salute to the unconscious figure. That seemed odd, too, because at camp he was not thought to be a really A-1 scout....

The two scoutmasters of the arriving troops remained in the bus with the first aid scouts and a queer little codger who seemed to be lame; the others walked. Hervey Willetts had ridden on top of that bus (contrary to orders), but he had never before lain quietly on the seat of it and been watched by two scoutmasters. He was always being watched by scoutmasters, but never in just this way....

So the old bus lumbered on. Soon he opened his eyes and mumbled something.

"Yes, my boy," said one of the scoutmasters; "what is it?"

"S—sma—smashed—br—," he said incoherently.

"Yes, we'll have a doctor as soon as we reach camp," the scoutmaster said soothingly. "Try to bear it. Don't move it and perhaps it won't pain so."

Hervey shook his head petulantly as if it were not his foot he spoke of. "Br—oken—the—br—look out——" And again he seemed to faint away.

The scoutmaster was puzzled.

In a few moments he spoke again, his eyes closed. But the word he spoke was clear.

"Ahead," he whispered.

The scoutmaster was still puzzled but he opened the bus door and called, "Gilbert, suppose you and a couple of the boys go on ahead and watch your step." Then to the other scoutmaster he said, "I think he's a bit delirious."

So it happened that it was Gilbert Tyson of the troop from Hillsburgh, forty or fifty miles down the line, who shouted to Darby Curren to stop, that the bridge had been washed away.

A funny part of the whole business was that the little duffer in the bus, who was attached to that troop, thought that Tyson was the hero of the occasion. He was strong on troop loyalty if on nothing else. So far as he was concerned (and he was very much concerned) Tyson had saved the lives of every scout in those two troops. Subsequent circumstances favored this delusion of his. For one thing, Hervey Willetts cared nothing at all about glory. You could not fit the mantle of heroism on him to save your life. He never talked about the affair, he was seldom at camp, except to sleep, and he did not know how he had managed the last few yards of his triumphal errand. For another thing, the Hillsburgh troop kept to themselves more or less, occupying one of the isolated "hill cabins." As for Tom Slade, he seldom talked much. He had seen too many stunts to lose his head over a new one, and he was a poor sort of publicity agent for Hervey.

Thus Goliath, as the little codger came to be known, had the field all to himself, and he turned out to be a mighty "hero maker."

CHAPTER X

PROVEN A SCOUT

The bus came to a stop a hundred feet or so from the ruined bridge and its passengers, going forward cautiously, looked down shudderingly into the yawning chasm. For a few seconds the very thought of what might have happened filled them with silent awe.

Goliath was the first to speak. "It's good Tyson saved our lives, isn't it?" he piped up. "We'd all be dead, 'wouldn't we?"

"Very dead," said one of the scouts; "so dead we probably wouldn't know it."

"Wouldn't know it?" asked Goliath, puzzled.

For answer the scout gave him a bantering push and tousled his hair for him. The little fellow took refuge with one of the scoutmasters.

"Will we get to that camp soon?" he asked.

"Pretty soon, I hope. Perhaps some one will come down and show us the way."

"Are we lost?"

"No, we're saved."

"I'm glad we're in Tyson's troop, aren't you?"

The scoutmaster laughed. "You bet," he said.

"Are there wild animals in that camp?"

"Scouts are all wild animals," the scoutmaster laughed again.

"Am I a wild animal?"

"Surest thing you know."

"Are you?"

"That's what."

"Is that fellow that's inside lying on the seat—is he dead?"

"No—not dead. But you mustn't go in and bother him."

The scene about the bridge was one of utter ruin. No vestige of the rustic structure was left; it had probably been carried away in the first overwhelming rush of water. The flood had subsided by now, and only a trickle of water passed through the gully. In this, and upon the sloping banks and the wreckage which had been Ebon Berry's garage, the scouts climbed about and explored the scene of devastation.

After a while a scoutmaster and several boys arrived from camp by way of the road. They had fought their way through mud and storm, bringing stretchers and a first aid kit, in expectation of finding disaster.

"This is not a very cheerful welcome to camp," one of the scoutmasters said. "The lake broke through up yonder. The boys have checked the flood with a kind of makeshift dam. We were afraid you had met with disaster. All safe and sound, are you?"

"Oh, yes, several of our boys went ahead and one of them shouted for us to stop——"

"That's the one right there," piped up the little fellow. "Maybe he'll get a reward, hey? Maybe he'll get a prize."

"I guess we're all safe and sound," said the other arriving scoutmaster; "but wet and hungry——"

"Especially hungry," one of the scouts said.

"That's a common failing here," said the man from camp.

"There's a funny fellow inside; want to see him?" piped up Goliath. "He hasn't got any clothes hardly, and he don't know what he's talking about; he hasn't got any conscience——"

"He means he's unconscious," said the scoutmaster. "We ran into him on the road. He really hasn't spoken yet, so we don't know anything about him. He seems a kind of victim of the storm—crazed. I think it just possible he intended—Come inside, won't you? I think we'll have to take him with us on a stretcher. I suppose he belongs in the countryside hereabouts."

Thus it was that Hervey's own scoutmaster looked down upon the unconscious form of his most troublesome and unruly scout. It was no wonder that the others had not thought him a scout. He looked more like a juvenile hobo. But sticking out of his soaking pocket was that one indubitable sign of identification, his rimless hat cut full of holes and decorated with its variety of badge buttons. Ruefully, Mr. Denny lifted this dripping masterpiece of original handiwork, and held it between his thumb and forefinger.

"This is one of our choicest youngsters," he said. "He is in my own troop. The last time I saw him, I explicitly told him not to leave camp without my permission. I suppose he has been on some escapade or other. I think he's about due for dismissal——"

"I don't think he's seriously injured, sir."

"Oh, no, he has a charmed life. Nine lives like a cat, in fact. Well, we'll cart him back."

"He doesn't look like a scout fellow," Goliath said.

"Well, he isn't what you would call a very good scout fellow, my boy," Mr. Denny said. "Good scout fellows usually know the law and obey it, if anybody should ask you."

"If they ask me, that's what I'll tell 'em," said Goliath, "hey?"

"You can't go far wrong if you tell them that," Mr. Denny said.

"And they have to save lives too, don't they?" the little codger piped up.

"Why, yes, you seem to have it all down pat," Mr. Denny said.

"We've got one of them in our troop," the little fellow said; "he's a hero."

"Well, I hope he reads the handbook and obeys the scout laws," said Mr. Denny significantly.

"I'm always going to have good luck," the little fellow said, rather irrelevantly. "I got a charm, too. Want to see it?"

"I think we'd better see if we can get to camp and find some hot stew," said Mr. Denny.

"That's the kind of a charm for me," said one of the scouts.

So it fell out that on this occasion, as on most others, Goliath was not permitted to dig down into the remote recess of his pocket to show that wonderful charm.

CHAPTER XI

THE NEW SCOUT

"Well," laughed Mr. Baxton, scoutmaster of the troop to which that little brownie of a boy belonged; "since we have a hero, we may as well use him. Suppose you stay here, Gilbert, and stop any vehicles that happen along."

"I think one of our boys from camp ought to do that," said one of the other scoutmasters. "How about you, Roy?"

The boy addressed was of a compact, natty build, with brown curly hair, and with the kind of smile which was positively guaranteed not to wash out in a storm. On his nose, which was of the aggressive and impudent type, were five freckles, set like the stars which form the big dipper, and his even teeth, which were constantly in evidence, were as white as snow. Across the bridge of his nose was a mark such as is seen upon the noses of persons who wear spectacles. But he wore no spectacles, though the imprint between his laughing, dancing eyes was said to have been caused by glasses—soda water glasses which were continually tipped up against his nose in obedience to the dictum that a scout shall be thorough.

"We'll both stay," he said; "if a Ford comes along we'll carry it across."

"Well, don't leave the spot, that's all," said Mr. Denny.

"Far be it from such," said Roy. "If we go away we'll take it with us. We should worry our young lives about a spot. Only save some stew for us. This night has been full of snap so far, it reminds me of a ginger-snap. We'll sit in one of those old cars, hey?"

Gilbert Tyson stared at Roy. He thought it wouldn't be half bad to stay here with this sprightly scout. The rest of the party, guided by Mr. Denny, started picking their way along the road to camp, carrying Hervey on a stretcher. Darby Curren, the stage-driver, doubtless tempted by the mention of hot stew, unharnessed his team and leaving the horses to graze in the adjacent field, accompanied the party. Roy and Gilbert Tyson watched the departing cavalcade till it was swallowed in darkness.

The rain had ceased now, and the wind was dying. In the sky was a little silvery break, and by its light flaky clouds were seen hurrying away, all in one direction like a flock of birds. It seemed as if they might be fleeing quietly from the wreck which they had caused.

"If one of the lights on those cars is working, we might use it for a signal," Roy said.

The cars of which he spoke were in the wreckage of Berry's garage. It had not been much of a garage, hardly more than a shack, in fact, and the two cars which now stood more or less damaged and exposed to the weather, had been its only contents, save for a work-bench and a few tools. Mr. Berry's flivver was quite beyond repair, having been overturned and carried some yards and apparently dashed against the bridge. There is no wreck in the world like the wreck of a Ford.

The heavier car had evidently withstood the first onrush of water and had made a stand against the flood, its wheels deep in the mud. This car was a roadster. Its side curtains were up, completely enclosing the single seat. It had evidently been used since the rainy weather started. It was not altogether free from damage, one of the fenders was bent, the bumper in front almost touched the ground on one side, an ornamental figurehead had been broken off the radiator cap, and the face of the radiator was dented. This car was equipped with a searchlight fastened on one end of the windshield, and as Gilbert Tyson handled this it lighted, sending a penetrating shaft of brightness into the night.

"It's funny the battery works after the soaking it got," said Roy. "Let's keep playing that light on the road. Anybody could see it half a mile off."

"Spell danger with it," Gilbert said.

"Sure, but I don't think anybody from camp will be along."

"You never can tell who knows the Morse Code and who doesn't," Gilbert said. "Keep playing it on the road, anyway."

The position of the car was such that this searchlight could be shown upon the road for perhaps the space of a quarter of a mile. It would have been quite sufficient to give pause to any approaching wagon or machine. Roy and Gilbert climbed into the car and sat upon the seat in the cosy enclosure formed by the curtains. It was quite pleasant in there. Since it was more agreeable to be fooling with the light than to let it shine steadily, Roy amused himself by spelling the word DANGER again and again.

Pretty soon one of the curtains opened and a voice said, "What's all the danger about?"

CHAPTER XII

THE GRAY ROADSTER

It was Tom Slade. With him was one of the best all-around scouts in camp, patrol leader of the Royal Bengal Tigers, Eagle Scout and winner of the Gold Cross, Bert Winton.

"What's this? The annual electrical show?" he asked. "What's the matter with you kids? Lost, strayed or stolen? Who's this fellow?"

"Look at the bridge, it's gone!" said Roy. "Don't bother to look at it. It isn't there anyway. We're a couple of pickets—I mean sentinels."

"Well, you guided us through the woods, anyway," said Tom.

"The pleasure is ours," said Roy. "We can sit in a car and guide people through the woods; we're real heroes. What's the news?"

"Do you know anything about the stage?" Tom asked.

"We know all about it. It's right over there. This fellow comes from Hillsburgh. He got out and walked ahead and stopped it. Didn't you? Hervey Willetts blew in from somewhere or other and they're carrying him to camp. Nothing serious. Got any candy?"

"The crowd from the bus is all right then?"

"Positively guaranteed."

"And Hervey?"

"He's used up another one of his lives, he's only got three left now. He must have hit the trail after Westy and I left the cove. He's going to get called down to-morrow. He should worry, he's used to that."

"Where did they run into him?" Tom asked.

"They found him hanging onto one of the horses. Curry thought he was a ghost, that's all I know. This fellow went ahead and shouted back that the bridge had sneaked off. Didn't you, Gilly?" It was characteristic of Roy that he had already found a nickname for Gilbert Tyson.

"Hervey say anything?"

"Mumbled something, I don't know what."

Tom pondered a few moments. "Humph," said he, "that's all right."

He was satisfied about Hervey. The other phases of the episode did not interest him. What scoutmasters said and thought did not greatly concern him. He did not give two thoughts to the fact that Hervey was to be "called down." He had known scouts to be called down before. He had known credit and glory to miscarry. Hervey had done this thing and that was all that the young camp assistant cared about. It would not hurt Hervey to be called down.

The picturesque young assistant, the very spirit and embodiment of adventure and romance, made a good deal of allowance for visiting scoutmasters and handbook scouts. He was broad and kind as the trees are broad and kind; exacting about big things, careless about little things. They knew all about scouting. He was the true scout. They had their manuals and handbooks. The great spirit of the woods was his. Hervey had made good. Why bother more about that?

So he just said, "Not hurt much, huh? Well, if you kids want to go up to camp, we'll take care of this job."

"Whose car is this, anyway?" asked Bert Winton. "I never saw it before. It's got bunged up a little, hey?"

Tom looked at the roadster rather interestedly, whistling to himself.

"It's gray," said Bert; "I never saw it before."

"It wasn't damaged in the flood," said Tom.

"Why wasn't it?" Roy demanded.

"Because it's facing down stream. Anything that hit it would have hit it in the back. I don't know whose it is, but it came here damaged, if you want to know."

"Sherlock Nobody Holmes, the boy detective," vociferated Roy. "We're not going to let it worry our innocent young lives, anyway, are we, Gilly? Oh, here comes somebody along the road! The plot grows thicker!"

Tom and Winton had cut through the woods, direct from the cove where they had been assisting in throwing together the makeshift dam. Fortunately the searchlight had made their journey easy. The figure which now approached along the road turned out to be Ebon Berry, owner of the wrecked garage, who had ventured forth from his home as soon as the storm had abated.

"Well, 'tain't no use cryin' over spilled milk, as the feller says," he observed as he contemplated the ruin all about him.

"You're about cleaned out, Mr. Berry," said Winton. "Whose car is this? I never saw it before."

"That? Well, now, that belongs to a feller that left it here, oh, I dunno, mebbe close onto a week ago. I ain't seed him since. Said he'd be back for it nex' day. I ain't seed nothin' of 'im. I guess that's what you'd call a racer, now, hain't it?"

"What are you going to do about it?" Tom asked. "It was damaged when it came here, wasn't it?"

"Yes, it were. Well, now, I don't jes' know what I'd auter do. Jes' nothin', I guess."

"'Tisn't going to do it any good buried here in the mud," Tom said.

"Well, 'tain't my loss, ony six dollars storage."

"Let's give it the once over," Tom said, in a way of half interest. The efforts of the night had been so strenuous that his casual interest in the car was something in the form of relaxation. It interested him as whittling a stick might have interested him. "Take a squint into that pocket there, Roy."

There was nothing but a piece of cotton waste in the flap pocket of the door nearest Roy, but Gilbert Tyson's ransacking of the other one revealed some miscellaneous paraphernalia; there was a pair of motorist's gloves, a road map, a newspaper, and two letters.

"Here, I'll give you the light," said Roy, as Tyson handed these things to Tom.

"You keep the light on the road," said Tom. "Let's have your flashlight."

"Now we're going to find out where the buried treasure lays hid—I mean hidden," said Roy. "We're going to unravel the mystery, as Pee-wee would say. 'Twas on a dark and stormy night——"

"Let's have your flashlight," said Tom, dryly.

CHAPTER XIII

THE UNKNOWN TRAIL

Gilbert Tyson and Roy sat in the car. Tyson had removed one curtain and Tom, standing close by, examined the papers in the glare of the flashlight which Tyson held. Bert Winton and Mr. Berry peered curiously over Tom's shoulder.

The map was of the usual folding sort, and on a rather large scale, showing the country for about forty or fifty miles roundabout.

"There's my little old home town," said Tyson, putting his finger on Hillsburgh, "home, sweet home."

"And here's little old Black Lake—before the flood," said Roy. "There's the camp, right there," he added, indicating the spot to Tyson; "there's where we eat, right there."

"And here's a trail up the mountain," said Tom. "See that lead pencil mark? You go up the back way. See?"

So there then was indeed a way up that frowning mountain opposite the camp. It was up the less precipitous slope, the slope which did not face the lake. The pencil marking had been made to emphasize the fainter printed line.

"Humph," said Tom, interested. "There's always some way up a mountain.... Maybe the light we saw up there ...let's have a squint at that letter, will you?"

"Have we got a right to read it?" Winton asked.

"We may be able to save a life by it," said Tom. "Sure."

But the letter did not reveal anything of interest. It was, in fact, only the last page of a letter which had been preserved on account of some trifling memorandums on the back of the sheet. What there was of the letter read as follows:

hope you will come back to England some time or other. I suppose America seems strange after all these years. You'll have to be content with shooting Indians and buffaloes now. But we'll save a fox or two for you. And don't forget how to ride horseback and we'll try not to forget about the rattle wagons.

REGGY.

"That's very kind of Reggy," said Roy. "Indians and buffaloes! Poor Indians. If he ever comes here, we'll teach him to shoot the shutes. If he's a good shot maybe we'll let him shoot the rapids."

"They all think America is full of Indians," said Winton.

"Indian pudding," said Roy; "mmm, mmm!"

"Well, let's see the newspaper," said Tom. "I don't suppose there's anything particular in that. Somebody that lived in England has been trying to go up the mountain—maybe. That's about all we know. We don't know that, even. But anyway, he hasn't come back."

"Maybe he's up there shooting Indians and buffaloes," said Roy. "We should worry."

"When was it he came here?" Tom asked.

"'Bout several days ago, I reckon," said Mr. Berry.

"That light's been up there all summer," Winton said.

"Until to-night," Tom added.

For a few moments no one spoke.

"Well, let's see the paper," said Tom, as he took it and began looking it over. He had not glanced at many of the headings when one attracted his attention. Following it was an article which he read carefully.

AUTOIST KILLS CHILD

Negligence and Reckless Driving Responsible for Accident

DRIVER ESCAPES

An accident which will probably prove fatal occurred on the road above Hillsburgh yesterday when a car described as a gray roadster ran down and probably mortally injured Willy Corbett, the eight-year-old son of Thomas Corbett of that place.

Two laborers in a nearby field, who saw the accident, say that the machine was running on the left side of the road where the child was playing and that but for this reckless violation of the traffic law, the little fellow would not have been run down. The driver was apparently holding to the left of the road, because the running was better there.

Exactly what happened no one seems to know. The autoist stopped, and started again, and when the two laborers had reached the spot where the child lay, the machine was going at the rate of at least forty miles an hour.

All efforts of town and county authorities to locate the gray roadster have failed.

"That's only about ten miles from where I live," said Gilbert Tyson.

Tom seemed to be thinking. "Let's look at that letter again," said he. "Humph," he added and handed it back to Roy.

"What?" Roy asked.

"Nothing," said Tom. "I guess this is the car all right."

"I don't see it," said Winton. "Just because it's a gray roadster — —"

"Well, there may be other little things about it, too," said Tom.

"About the car or the letter or what?" Winton asked.

"Answered in the affirmative," said Roy.

"Well, anyway," Tom said, "it looked as if the owner of the car might have gone up the mountain. And he hasn't come down. At least he hasn't come after his car. I'd like to get a look at him. I'm going to follow that trail up a ways — —"

"To-night?"

"When did you suppose? Next week? I'd like to find out where the trail goes. I'm not saying any more. The bright spot we saw from camp went out to-night. And here's a trail on the other side of the mountain that I never knew of. Here's a man that had a map of it and he went away and hasn't come back. I'm not asking anybody to go with me."

"And I'm not asking you to let me," said Roy. "I'll go just for spite. You don't think you're afraid of me, am I, quoth he. Now that we're here, we might as well be all separated together. What do you say, Gilly? Yes, kind sir, said he. We'll all go, what do you say? Indeed we will, they answered joyously — — "

"Well, come ahead then," said Tom, "and stop your nonsense."

"Says you," Roy answered.

CHAPTER XIV

ON THE SUMMIT

The two facts uppermost in Tom's mind were these: Some one had marked the trail up that mountain, and the patch of brightness on the top of the mountain which had lately been familiar to the boys in camp had that very night disappeared.

The owner of the gray roadster had not come back for it. He might be the fugitive of the newspaper article, and he might not. If Tom had anyparticular reason for thinking that he was, he did not say so. There are a good many gray roadsters. One thing which puzzled Tom was this: the car had been in storage at Berry's for a few days at the very most, but the bright patch on the mountain had been visible for a month or more. So if the owner of this machine had gone up the mountain, at least he was not the originator of the bright patch there. But perhaps, after all, the bright patch was just some reflection.

SUDDENLY ROY CALLED, "LOOK HERE! HERE'S A BOARD!"

Tom Slade's Double Dare.   Page 83

"Let's have another look at that letter," said Tom.

He read it again with an interest and satisfaction which certainly were not justified by the simple wording of the missive.

"Come ahead," he said; "we can't get much wetter than we are already. We might as well finish the night's work. I guess Mr. Berry'll take care of the searchlight."

Mr. Berry had no intention of leaving the scene of his ruined possessions to the mercy of vandals. Moreover, it seemed likely that with the abatement of the storm the neighboring village would turn out to view the devastation.

Once the end of the trail was located, the ascent of the mountain was not difficult, and the four explorers made their way up the comparatively easy slope, hindered only by trees which had fallen across the path. The old mountain which frowned so forbiddingly down upon the camp across the lake was very docile when taken from behind. It was just a big bully.

As Tom and the three scouts approached the summit, the devastation caused by the storm became more and more appalling. Great trees had been torn up as if they had been no more than house plants. These had fallen, some to the ground and some against other trees, their spreading roots dislodging big rocks which had gone crashing down against other trees. Some of these rocks remained poised where the least agitation would release them.

Nature cannot be disturbed like this without suffering convulsions afterwards, and the continual low noises of dripping roots and of trees and branches sinking and settling and falling from temporary supports, gave a kind of voice of suffering and anguish to the wilderness.

These strange sounds were on every hand and they made the wrecked and drenched woods to seem haunted. Now and again a sound almost human would startle the cautious wayfarers as they picked their way amid the sodden chaos. In places it seemed as if the merest footfall would dislodge some threatening bowlder which would blot their lives out in a second. And the ragged, gaping chasms left by roots made the soggy ground uncertain support for yards about.

Toward the summit the path was quite obliterated under the jumble of the wreckage, and the party clambered over and threaded their way amid this débris until the tiny but cheering lights of Temple Camp were visible far down across the lake. There the two arriving troops were about finishing their hot stew! Far down and nearer than the camp was a moving speck of light; some one was on the lake. The boys did not venture too near that precipitous descent.

Suddenly Roy, who had been walking along a fallen tree trunk, called, "Look here! Here's a board!"

He had hauled it out from under the trunk, and the others, approaching, looked at it with interest. In all that wild desolation there was something very human about a fragment of board. Somehow it connected that unknown wilderness with the world of men.

"That didn't come up here by itself," said Tom.

"You're right, it didn't," said Tyson.

"Here's a rusty nail in it," Roy added.

The board, unpainted and weather beaten as it was, seemed singularly out of place in that remote forest.

Suddenly Roy grasped Tom's arm; his hand trembled; his whole form was agitated.

"Look!" he whispered hoarsely. "Look—down there—right there. See? Do you see it? Right under.... Oh, boy, it's awful...."

CHAPTER XV

A SCOUT IS THOROUGH

Scout though he was, Roy's hand trembled as he passed his flashlight to Tom. He could not, for his life, point that flashlight himself at the grewsome object which he had seen in the darkness.

Lying crossways underneath the trunk was the body of a man, his face looking straight up into the sky with a fixed stare, and a soulless grin upon his ashen face. Somewhere nearby, mud was dripping from an exposed root, and the earth laden drops as they fell one by one into the ragged cavity gave a sound which simulated a kind of unfeeling laughter. It seemed as if that stark, staring thing might be chuckling through its rigid, grinning mouth. Roy's weight and movement on the trunk communicated a slight stir to the ghastly figure and its head moved ever so little....

"No," said Tom, anticipating Winton's question; "he's dead. Get off the log, Roy."

"Well, I wish that dripping would stop, anyway," said Winton.

Tom approached the figure, the others following and standing about in silence as he examined it. They all avoided the log, the slightest movement of which had an effect which made them shudder.

Raising one cold, muddy hand, Tom felt the wrist, laying it gently down again. There was not even a faint, departing vestige of life in the trapped, crushed body.

"Is it him?" Gilbert Tyson asked in a subdued tone.

"Guess so," said Tom, kneeling.

The others stood back in a kind of fearful respect, watching, waiting.... Now and then a leaf or twig fell. And once, some broken tree limb crackled as it adjusted itself in its fallen estate. And all the while the mud kept dripping, dripping, dripping....

Lying on the dead man's open coat, as if they had fallen from his pocket, were two cards and a letter. These Tom picked up and glanced at, using Roy's flashlight. One of the cards was an automobile registration card. The other was a driver's license card. They were both of the State of New Jersey and issued to Aaron Harlowe. The letter had been stamped but not mailed. It was addressed to Thomas Corbett, North Hillsburgh, New York. This name tallied with the name of the child's father in the newspaper.

Here was pretty good proof that the man who had met death here upon this wild, lonely mountain was none other than the owner of the gray roadster, the coward who had fled from the consequences of his negligence, and turned it into a black crime!

"Are you going to open it?" Bert Winton asked.

"I guess no one has a right to do that but the coroner," Tom said. "We have no right to move the body even."

"Well," said Bert Winton, his awe at the sight of death somewhat subsiding at thought of the victim's cowardice, "there's an end of Aaron Harlowe who ran over Willie Corbett with a gray roadster and — — "

"And was going to send a letter to the kid's father," concluded Tom. "And here's his footprint, too. I'd like to take his shoe off and fit it into this footprint," Tom said.

"What for?" Roy asked.

"Just to make sure."

But Tom soon dismissed that thought and the others did not relish it. Moreover, Tom knew that the law prohibited him from doing such a thing.

With the mystery, as it seemed, cleared up, there remained nothing to do but explore the immediate vicinity for the sake of scout thoroughness. Their search revealed other loose boards, a few cooking utensils and finally the utter wreck of what must have been a very primitive and tiny shack. This was perhaps a couple of hundred feet from the body and below the highest point of the mountain. It was conceivable that a fire here might have shown in a faint glare down at camp. The blaze could not have been seen. Amid the ruin of the shack were a few rough cooking utensils. The soaking land and the darkness effectually concealed the charred remnants of any fire.

"Well, he'll never shoot any buffaloes and wild Indians," said Roy.

Tom replaced the cards and letter, or rather put them in the dead man's pocket for fear the wind might blow them away, though being under the lee of the trunk they had been somewhat protected. Then the party retraced their path down the mountain and, circling its lower reaches, found themselves at last upon the lake shore.

Thus ended the work of that fretful night, a night ever memorable at Temple Camp, a night of death and devastation. The mighty wind which smote the forest and drove the ruinous waters before it, died in the moment of its triumph. The sodden, sullen heaven which had cast its gloom and poured its unceasing rain, rain, rain, upon the camp for two full weeks, cleared and the edges of the departing clouds were bathed in the silver moonlight. And the next morning the bright, merry sun arose and smiled down upon Temple Camp and particularly on Goliath who sat swinging his legs from the springboard.

CHAPTER XVI

THE WANDERING MINSTREL

He was defying, single handed, half a dozen or more scouts who were flopping about in rowboats under and about the springboard. They had just rowed across after an inspection of the washed-out cove, and were resting on their oars, jollying the little fellow whose legs dangled above them.

"Where did that big feller go?" he asked.

"To the village."

"He found a dead man last night, didn't he?"

"That's what he did."

"I know his name, it's Slade."

"Right the first time. You're a smart fellow."

"I like that big feller. He says Gilbert Tyson is all right; I asked him. I bet Gilbert Tyson can beat any of you fellers. He's in my troop, he is. I bet you were never in a hospital."

"I bet you were never in prison," a scout ventured.

"I bet you never got hanged," Goliath piped up.

"I bet I did," another scout said.

"When?"

"To-morrow afternoon."

"To-morrow afternoon isn't here yet," Goliath said, triumphantly.

"Sure it is, this is to-morrow afternoon. Somebody told me yesterday. If it was to-morrow afternoon yesterday it must be to-day."

"Posolutely," said Roy Blakeley. "What was true yesterday is true to-day, because the truth is always the same—only different."

"Sure," concurred another scout, "to-morrow, to-day will be yesterday. It's as clear as mud."

Goliath thought for a few moments and then made a flank attack.

"Gilbert Tyson is a hero," he said; "he saved the lives of everybody in that bus — he did."

"That's where he was wrong," said Roy Blakeley; "a scout is supposed to be generous. He mustn't be all the time saving."

"Isn't it good to save lives?" Goliath demanded.

"Sure, but not too many. A scout that's all the time saving gets to be stingy."

Goliath pondered a moment.

"Gilly is all right but he's not a first-class scout," said Roy.

"A first-class scout," said Westy Martin, "is not supposed to turn back. Gilbert turned back. Then he shouted 'stop.' Law three says that a scout is courteous. He should have said 'please stop.' Law ten says that a scout must face danger, but he turned his back to it. He wasn't thinking about the danger, all he was thinking about was the bus. All he was thinking about was being thrifty — saving lives. I've known fellows like that before. It's just like striking an average; a scout that strikes an average is a coward."

"You mean if the average is small?" said Roy.

"Oh, sure."

"Because it all depends," Roy continued; "a scout isn't supposed to fight, is he? But he can strike an attitude. The same as he can hit a trail. Suppose he hits a poor, little thin trail— —"

"Then he's a coward," said Connie Bennett.

"Not necessarily," said Westy, "because— —"

"A scout has to be obedient! You can't deny that!" Goliath nearly fell off the springboard in his excitement. "That other feller is going to get sent away because I heard a man say so!"

This was not exactly an answer to the well-reasoned arguments of Roy and his friends, but it had the effect of making them serious. Moreover, just at that juncture, Mr. Carroll, scoutmaster of the Hillsburgh troop, appeared and very gently ordered Goliath from his throne upon the springboard. The little fellow's mind had been somewhat unsettled by the skillful reasoning of his new friends. He trotted off in obedience to Mr. Carroll's injunction that he go in and take off his wet shoes.

"Boys," said the new scoutmaster, in a pleasant, confidential tone which won all, "I want to say a word to you about the little brownie we have with us. You'll find him an odd little duck. I'm hoping to make a scout of him some time or other. Meanwhile, we have to be careful not to get him excited. It's a rule of our troop to take with us camping each summer, some little needy inmate of an orphan home or hospital or some place of the sort, and give him the benefit of the country air. This little fellow is our charge this year. You won't talk to him about his past, because we want him to forget that. We want to take him home well and strong and I look to you for help. Make friends with him and get him interested in things about camp. His heart isn't strong; be careful."

Good scouts that they were, they needed no more than these few words. Temple Camp usually took new boys as it found them, anyway, concerning itself with their actions and not with the history of their lives. Half the scouts in the big summer community didn't know where the other half came from, and cared less. From every corner of the land they came and all they knew or cared about each other was limited to their intercourse at camp.

"You don't suppose that's true, do you?" one of them asked when Mr. Carroll had gone.

"What? About Willetts?"

"Sure."

"Dare say. He's about due for the G. B., I guess. But if you want to cook a fish you've got to catch him first."

"Where is he, anyway?" one asked. "I thought his foot was so bad."

"I saw him limping off this morning, that's all I know," another said.

"It would take more than a lame ankle to keep him at camp," said Dorry Benton of Roy's patrol. "Did you see that crazy stick he was using for a cane?"

"The wandering minstrel," another scout commented.

"He stands pat with Slady, all right."

"Gee, you can't help liking the fellow."

"I have to laugh at him," Westy said.

"You can't pal with him, that's one thing," another observed.

"That's because you can't keep up with him; even Mr. Denny has a sneaky liking for him."

"Do you know what one of his troop told me? He told me he always wears that crazy hat to school when he's home. Some nut!"

"Reckless, happy-go-lucky, that's what he is."

"Come on over and let's look on the bulletin board."

They all strolled, half idly, to the bulletin board which stood outside the main pavilion. It was a rule of camp that every scout should read the announcements there each afternoon. Then there would be no excuse for ignorance of important matters pertaining to camp plans. Upon the board were tacked several announcements, a hike for the morrow, letters uncalled for, etc. Conspicuous among these was the following:

Hervey Willetts will report immediately to his scoutmaster at troop's cabin, upon his arrival at camp.

WM. C. DENNY.

CHAPTER XVII

TOM'S INTEREST AROUSED

On that same day a solemn little procession picked its way carefully down the trail from the storm-wrecked summit of the mountain. Four of the county officials bore a stretcher over which was tied a white sheet. With the party was Tom Slade who had guided the authorities to the grewsome discovery of the previous night. In this work, and in the subsequent assistance which he rendered, he was absent from camp throughout the day. This unpleasant business had not been advertised in camp.

Of the tragic end of Aaron Harlowe nothing more was known. Several days previously he had come to the neighborhood in his gray roadster, a fugitive, with the stigma of cowardice upon his conscience. He had tried to compromise with his conscience, as it appeared, by enclosing a sum of money in an envelope and addressing it to the father of the child he had run down. But his death had prevented the mailing of this. The telltale finger of accusation was pointed at him from the newspaper which was in his car.

His identity was established to the satisfaction of the authorities by the name upon the license and registration cards found with his body. Why he had ascended the mountain and remained there several days only to be crushed to death in the storm, no one could guess. The conclusion of the authorities was that he was crazed by fear and remorse. This seemed not improbable, for his weak attempt to make amends with money showed him to be not altogether bad.

With the taking of the body by the authorities, Tom's participation in the tragic business ended. Yet there were one or two things which stuck in his mind and puzzled him. There had been a light on the mountain before ever this Harlowe had gone up there. There had been a crude shack near the summit. The light had disappeared amid the storm. The boys, watching the storm from the pavilion, had seen the light disappear. Did Harlowe, therefore, climb the mountain to escape man or to seek man? Harlowe's life went out in that same tempestuous hour when the light went out. But how came the light there? And where was the originator of it?

One rather odd question Tom asked the authorities and got very little satisfaction from them. "Do you notice any connection between that article in the newspaper and the letter the dead man got from England?" he asked.

"No manner uv connection; leastways none as I kin see," said the sheriff. "The paper showed what he done; the map showed whar he went; the license cards showed who he was. And thar ye are, sonny, whole thing sure's gospel."

"It's funny about the light," said Tom, respectfully.

"I ain't botherin' my head 'baout no lights, son. I found Aaron Harlowe 'n that's enough, hain't it?"

It was in Tom's thoughts to say, "You didn't find him, I found him." But out of respect for the formidable badge which the sheriff wore on one strand of his suspenders, he refrained.

The next morning the newspapers told with conspicuous headlines, the tragic sequel of Aaron Harlowe's escape. "Found on lonely mountain," they said. "Fugitive motorist killed in storm," one of the write-ups was headed: "Storm wreaks vengeance on autoist," which was one of the best headings of the lot. "Sheriff's posse makes grewsome find" was another. And all told how Aaron Harlowe, fleeing guiltily from his crime, had met his fate in the storm-tossed wilds of that frowning mountain. They dwelt on the justice of Providence; they made the storm a kind of avenging hero. It was pretty good stuff.

And that, as I said in the beginning, was where the public interest in Aaron Harlowe ended. The rest of the strange business was connected with Temple Camp and the scouts, and never got into the papers....

It was exactly like Tom Slade that something should interest him in this tragic episode which did not interest the authorities. He left them, quite unsatisfied in his own mind, and with some kind of a bee in his bonnet....

CHAPTER XVIII

TRIUMPH AND— —

At about the time that Tom was starting back to camp, rather thoughtful and preoccupied, Hervey Willetts was arriving at camp, not at all thoughtful or preoccupied.

His ankle was strained and bruised, and he limped. But his rimless hat of many holes and button-badges was perched sideways toward the back of his head and had a new and piquant charm by reason of being faded and water soaked. Putting not his trust in garters, which had so often, betrayed him, he had fastened a string to his left stocking by means of an old liberty loan pin. The upper end of this string was tied to a stick which he carried over his shoulder, so he had only to exert a little pressure on the stick in front to adjust his stocking.

He had evidently been to see one of his farmer friends, for he was eating a luscious red tomato, and fate decreed that the last of this should be ready for consumption just as he was passing within a few yards of the bulletin board. For a moment a terrible conflict raged within him. Should he despatch the remainder of the tomato into his mouth, or at the bulletin board? The small remnant was red and mushy and dripping—and the bulletin board won.

Brandishing the squashy missile, he uttered his favorite passwords to good luck,

One for courage

One for spunk

One to take aim

And then— —

Suddenly he bethought him of an improvement. Sticking the remnant of tomato on the end of his stick, he swung it carefully.

One for courage

One for spunk

One to take aim

And then — KERPLUNK!

Those magic words were intended, especially, for use in despatching tomatoes and they never failed to make good. There, upon the bulletin board was a vivid area which looked like the midday sun. From it trickled an oozy mass, down over the list of uncalled for letters, straight through the prize awards of yesterday, obliterating the Council Call, and bathing the list of new arrivals in soft and pulpy red. The "hike for to-morrow," as shown, was through a crimson sea.

Hervey approached for a closer glimpse of his triumph. No other incentive would have taken him so close to that prosy bulletin board. He had vaulted over it but never read it. But now in the moment of supreme victory he limped forward, like an elated artist, to inspect his work.

There, in front of him, with a little red river flowing down across the middle of it, was the ominous sentence.

Hervey Willetts will report immediately to his scoutmaster at troop's cabin, upon his arrival at camp.

WM. C. DENNY.

CHAPTER XIX

HERVEY SHOWS HIS COLORS

"If I hadn't fired the tomato I wouldn't have known about that," said Hervey. Which fact, to him, fully justified the juicy bombardment. "That shows how you never can tell what's going to happen next." And this was certainly true of Hervey.

But to do him justice, what was going to happen next never worried him. He took things as they came. He was not the one to sidestep an issue. The ominous notice signed by his scoutmaster had the effect of directing his ambling course to that officer's presence, on which detour, he might encounter new adventures. To reach his troop's cabin he would have to pass the cooking shack where a doughnut might be speared with a stick. All was for the best. He would as lief go to troop cabin as anywhere else....

In this blithe and carefree spirit, he approached the rustic domicile which he seldom honored by his presence, singing one of those snatches of a song which were the delight of camp, and which rounded out his rôle of wandering minstrel:

Oh, there is no place like the old camp-fire,

As all the boy scouts know;

And the best little place is home, sweet home —

When there isn't any other place to go, go, go.

When there isn't any other place to go.

Mr. Denny, standing in the doorway of the cabin, contemplated him with a repressed smile. "Hervey," he could not help saying, "since you think so well of the camp-fire, I wonder you don't choose to see more of it."

"I can see it from all the way across the lake," said Hervey. "I can see it no matter where I go."

"I see. It must arouse fond thoughts. I'm afraid, Hervey, to quote your own song, there isn't any other place for you to go but home, sweet home. You seem to have exhausted all the places. Sit down, Hervey, you and I have got to have a little talk."

Hervey leaned against the cabin, Mr. Denny sat upon the door sill. None of the troop was about; it was very quiet. For half a minute or so Mr. Denny did not speak, only whittled a stick.

"I sometimes wonder why you joined the scouts, Hervey," he said. "Your disposition— —"

"A fellow that sat next to me in school dared me to," said Hervey.

"Oh, it was a sort of a wager?"

"I wouldn't take a dare from anybody."

"And so you joined as a stunt?"

"I heard that scouts jumped off cliffs and all like that."

"I see. Well, now, Hervey, I've written to your father that I'm sending you home."

Hervey began making rings in the soil with his stick but said nothing. Mr. Denny's last words were perhaps a little more than he expected, but he gave no other hint of his feelings.

And so for another minute or so there was silence, except for the distant voices of some scouts out upon the lake.

"It is not exactly as a punishment, Hervey; it is just that I can't take the responsibility, that's all. You see?"

"Y— — yes, sir."

"I thought you would. Your father thought the influence of camp would be good, but you see you are seldom at camp. We can't help you because we can't find you."

"You can't cook a fish till you catch it," said Hervey.

"That's just it, Hervey."

"If you don't want to leave any tracks the best thing is to swing into trees every now and then," Hervey informed him.

"Ah, I see. Now, Hervey, my boy, I'm anxious that you and I should understand each other. You have done nothing disgraceful and I don't think you ever will — —"

"I landed plunk on my head once."

"Well, that was more of a misfortune than a disgrace."

"It hurt like the dickens."

"I suppose it did."

Mr. Denny paused; he was up against the hardest job he had ever tackled. It was harder than he had thought it would be.

"You see, Hervey, how it is. Last week you stayed away over night at some farm. I had told you you must not leave camp without my knowledge. For that I had you stay here all day, making a birchbark basket. I thought that was a good punishment."

"I'll tell the world it was," said Hervey.

Mr. Denny paused before proceeding.

"Did it do any good? Not a bit."

"The basket was a punk one," said Hervey.

"Again you rode down as far as Barretstown, hitching onto a freight train."

"I'd have got all the way down to Jonesville, if it hadn't been for the conductor. He was some old grouch, believe me."

"Then we had a little talk — you remember. You promised to be here at meal times. Look at Mr. Ellsworth's troop, Harris, Blakeley and those boys. Always on hand for meals — —"

"I'll say so; they're some hungry bunch," Hervey commented.

"And you gave me your word that you wouldn't leave camp without my permission. You think as little about breaking your word as you do aboutbreaking your leg, Hervey," Mr. Denny added with sober emphasis.

Hervey began poking the ground again with his stick.

"That's just the truth, Hervey. And it can't go on any longer."

"Am I out of the troop?" Hervey asked, wistfully.

"N—no, you're not. But I want you to learn to be as good a scout in one way as you are in another. You have won merit badges with an ease which is surprising to me——"

"They're a cinch," Hervey interrupted.

"I want you to go home and stop doing stunts and read the handbook. I want you to read the oath and the scout laws, so that when the rest of us come home you can give me your hand and say, 'I'm an all round scout, not just a doer of stunts.'"

"H—how soon are—the rest of you coming back?" Hervey asked with just the faintest suggestion of a break in his voice.

"Why, you know we're here for six weeks, Hervey. Don't you know anything about your troop's affairs? You know how much money we have in our treasury, don't you?"

Hervey did not miss the reproach. He said nothing, only kept tracing the circle with his stick. Finally it occurred to him to mark two eyes, a nose and a mouth in the circle. Mr. Denny sat studying him. I think Mr. Denny was on the point of weakening. Hervey seemed sober and preoccupied. But the face on the ground seemed to wink at Mr. Denny as if to intercede in its young creator's behalf.

Mr. Denny gathered his strength as one does on the point of taking an unpalatable medicine.

"Yesterday, Hervey, I expressly reminded you of your promise not to leave camp. I did that because I thought the storm might tempt you forth."

"They call me — —"

"Yes, I know; they call you the stormy petrel. You went across the lake with others. They returned but you did not return with them. Where you went I don't know. And I'm not going to ask you, Hervey, for it makes no difference. I understand young Mr. Slade was there, but that makes no difference. Blakeley and one of his troop, Westy Martin, reached camp and reported conditions in the cove — —"

"He's all right, Blakeley is — —"

"Hours passed, no one knew where you were. I was too proud, or too ashamed, to go and ask Slade if he knew. I am jealous of our troop's reputation, Hervey — even if you are not — —"

Hervey leaned against the cabin, looking abstractedly at his handiwork on the ground.

"There was great confusion and excitement here," Mr. Denny continued. "The whole camp turned out to save the lake, to stem the flood. But you were not here. Your companions in our troop worked till they were dog tired. But where were you? Helping? No, you were off on some vagabond journey — disobedient, insubordinate."

Mr. Denny spoke with resolute firmness now and his voice rang as he uttered his scathing accusations.

"You were a traitor not only to your troop, but to the camp — the camp which held out the hand of good fellowship to you when you came here. A slacker — —"

Hervey broke his stick in half and threw it on the ground. His breast heaved. He looked down. He said nothing. Mr. Denny studied him curiously for a few seconds.

"That is the truth, Hervey. One wrong always produces another. You were disobedient and insubordinate, and that led to — what?"

Hervey gulped, but whether in shame or remorse or what, Mr. Denny could not make out, He was to know presently.

"It led to shirking, whether intentional or not. And to-night, because there is no train, you are going to sleep in the camp which you deserted. You will, perhaps, row on the lake which others have saved for you. You see it now in its true light, don't you? You had better go and thank Blakeley and his comrade for what they did, if you have any real feeling for the camp."

"I— —"

"Don't speak. Nothing you could say would make a difference, Hervey. I know from Mr. Carroll and his boys where you showed up. I know they found you clinging to one of the stage horses. I was there later and saw you. You might have been plunged into that chasm with all the rest of them and been crushed to pieces, if one of those scouts hadn't gone ahead, as he was told to do, and if he hadn't kept his mind on what he had been told to do, instead of disregarding his scoutmaster and— —"

He paused, for Hervey was shaking perceptibly. He watched the boy curiously. Should he go on with this thing and see it through? He summoned his resolution.

"No, Hervey, as I said, I have written to your father. I have said nothing against you, only that you are too much for me here, where my responsibility is great. I want you to get your things together and take the train in the morning. We'll expect to see you when we come home. There is no hard feeling, Hervey. When we come home you're going to start all over again, my boy, and learn the thing right. You— —"

With a kind of spasmodic effort Hervey raised his head and, with a pride there was no mistaking, looked his scoutmaster straight in the face. He was trembling visibly. If there was any contrition in his countenance, Mr. Denny did not see it. He was quite taken aback with the fine show of spirit which his young delinquent showed. There was even a dignity in the old cap with its holes and badges, as it sat perched on the side of his head. There was a touch of pathos, even of dignity too, in his fallen stocking.

"I—I—wouldn't stay here—now—I wouldn't—I—not even if you asked me—I wouldn't. I wouldn't even if you—if you got down on your knees and begged me——"

"Hervey, my boy——"

"No, I won't listen. I—I wouldn't stay even to-night—I wouldn't. Do you think I need a train? I—I can hike to Jonesville, can't I? You say I'm—I'm no scout—Tom Slade he said——"

"Hervey——"

"I don't—anyhow—I don't care anything about the rest of them. I wouldn't stay even for supper. Even if you—if you apologized—I wouldn't——"

"Apologize? Why, Hervey——"

"For what you said—called me—I wouldn't. I don't give a—a—damn—I don't—for all the people here—only except one—and I wouldn't stay if you got down on your knees and begged me—I wouldn't——"

Mr. Denny contemplated him with consternation in every feature. There was no stopping him. The accused had become the accuser. There was something stirring, something righteous, in this fine abandon. In the setting of the outburst of hurt pride even the profane word seemed to justify itself. The tables were completely turned and Hervey Willetts was master of the situation.

CHAPTER XX

TOM ADVISES GOLIATH

It was late afternoon when Tom Slade, tramping home after his day spent with the minions of the law, crossed the main road and hit into the woods trail which afforded a short cut to camp.

It was the laziest hour of the day, the gap between mid afternoon and supper time. It was a tranquil time, a time of lolling under trees and playing the wild game of mumbly-peg, and of jollying tenderfoots, and waiting for supper. Roy Blakeley always said that the next best thing to supper was waiting for it. The lake always looked black in that pre-twilight time when the sun was beyond though not below the summit of the mountain. It was the time of new arrivals. In that mountain-surrounded retreat they have two twilights—a tenderfoot twilight and a first class twilight. It was the time when scouts, singly and in groups, came in from tracking, stalking and what not, and sprawled about and got acquainted.

But there was one who did not come in on that peaceful afternoon, and that was the wandering minstrel. If Tom Slade had crossed the main road ten minutes sooner, he might have seen that blithe singer going along the road, but not with a song on his lips. The sun of that carefree nature was under a cloud. But his loyal stocking kept descending, and his suit-case dangled from a stick over his shoulder. His trick hat perched jauntily upon his head, Hervey Willetts was himself again. Not quite, but almost. At all events he did not ponder on the injustice of the world and the cruelty of fate. He was wondering whether he could make Jonesville in time for the night train or whether he had better try for the boat at Catskill Landing. The boat had this advantage, that he could shinny up the flagpole if the pilot did not see him. The train offered nothing but the railing on the platforms ...

If Tom had been ten minutes earlier!

The young camp assistant left the trail and hit down through the grove and around the main pavilion. The descending sun shone right in his face as he neared the lake. It made his brown skin seem almost like that of a mulatto. His sleeves were rolled up as they always were, showing brown muscular arms, with a leather wristlet (but no watch) on one. His pongee shirt was open almost down to his waist. His faded khaki trousers were held up by a heavy whip lash drawn tight around his waist.

Not a single appurtenance of the scout was upon him. He was rather tall, and you who have known him as a hulking youngster with bull shoulders will be interested to know that he had grown somewhat slender and exceedingly lithe. He had that long stride and silent footfall which the woods life develops. He was still tow-headed, though he fixed his hair on occasions, which is saying something. You would have been amused at his air of quiet assurance. Perhaps he had not humor in the same sense that Roy Blakeley had, but he had an easy, bantering way which was captivating to the scouts.

Dirty little hoodlum that he once was, he was now the most picturesque, romantic figure in the camp. In Tom Slade, beloved old Uncle Jeb, camp manager, seemed to have renewed his own youth. Scouts worshipped at the shrine of this young confidant of the woods, trustees consulted him, scoutmasters respected him.

As he emerged around the corner of the storage cabin, several scouts who had taken their station within inhaling distance of the cooking shack fell in with him and trotted along beside him.

"H'lo, Slady, can we go with you?"

"I'm going to wash my hands," said Tom, giving one of them a shove.

"Good night! I don't want to go."

"I thought you wouldn't."

In Tent Avenue the news of his passing got about and presently a menagerie of tenderfoots were dogging his heels.

"Where you been, Slady? Can I go? Take me? Take us on the lake, Slady?"

As he passed the two-patrol cabins Goliath slid down from the woodpile and challenged him. "Hey, big feller, I got a souvenir. Want to see it? I know who you are; you're boss, ain't you?"

"H'lo, old top," said Tom, tousling his hair for him. "Well, how do you think you like Temple Camp?"

Goliath had hard work to keep up with him, but he managed it.

"I had two pieces of pie," he said.

"Good for you."

"Maybe I'll get to be a regular scout, hey?"

"Not till you can eat six pieces."

"Were you ever in a hospital?"

"Yop, over in France."

"I bet you licked the Germans, didn't you?"

"Oh, I had a couple of fellows helping me."

"A fellow in my troop is a hero; he's going to get a badge, maybe. A lot of fellers said so."

"That's the way to do," said Tom.

"His name is Tyson, that's what his name is. Do you know him?"

"You bet."

"He saved all the fellers in that wagon from getting killed because he shouted for the wagon to stop. So he's a hero, ain't he?"

"Well, I don't know about that," said Tom cheerily; "medals aren't so easy to get."

"There was a crazy feller near that wagon. I bet you were never crazy, were you?"

"Not so very."

"Will you help him to get the medal—Tyson?"

"Well, now, you let me tell you something," said Tom; "don't you pay so much attention to these fellows around camp. The main thing for you to do is to eat pie and stew and things. A lot of these fellows think it's easy to get medals. And they think it's fun to jolly little fellows like you. Don't you think about medals; you think about dinner."

"But after I get through thinking about dinner— —"

"Then think about supper. You can't eat medals."

Goliath seemed to ponder on this undesirable truth. He soon fell behind and presently deserted Tom to edify a group of scouts near the boat landing.

Of course, Tom did not take seriously what Goliath had said about awards. He knew Tyson and he knew that Tyson would be the last one in the world to pose as a hero. But he also knew something of the disappointments which innocent banter and jollying had caused in camp. He knew that the wholesome spirit of fun in Roy Blakeley and others had sometimes overreached itself, causing chagrin. There was probably nothing to this business at all but, for precaution's sake, he would nip it in the bud.

One incidental result of his little chat with Goliath was that he was reminded of Hervey's exploit, a matter which he had entirely forgotten in his more pressing preoccupations. Tom was no hero maker and he knew that Hervey would only trip on the hero's mantle if he wore it. As time had gone on in camp, Tom had found himself less and less interested in the pomp and ceremony and theatrical clap-trap of awards. Bravery was in the natural course of things. Why make a fuss about it?

For that very reason, he was not going to have any heads turned with rapturous dreams of gold and silver awards. He was not going to have any new scouts' visit blighted by vain hopes. He did not care greatly about awards, but he cared a good deal about the scouts ...

CHAPTER XXI

WORDS

After he had prepared for supper he went up the hill to the cabin occupied by Mr. Carroll's troop. It was pleasantly located on a knoll and somewhat removed from the main body of camp. Mr. Carroll was himself about to start down for supper.

"H'lo, Mr. Carroll," said Tom; "alone in your glory?"

"The boys have gone down," said Mr. Carroll. "They'll be sorry to have missed a visit from Tom Slade."

"Comfortable?" Tom asked.

"Couldn't be more so, thank you. We can almost see home from up here, though the boys prefer not to look in that direction."

Tom glanced about. "Sometimes new troops are kind of backward to ask for things," he said. "We're not mind readers, you know. So sing out if there's anything you want."

"Thank you."

"Kid comfortable?"

"Yes, he's giving his attention to pie and awards."

"Hm," said Tom, seating himself on a stump. "Pie's all right, but you want to have these fellows go easy on awards. The boys here in camp are a bunch of jolliers. Of course, you know the handbook——"

"Oh, yes."

"And you know Tyson doesn't stand to win any medal for anything he did last night. Strictly speaking, he saved your lives, I suppose, but it isn't exactly a case for an award."

"Oh, mercy, no."

"I'm glad you see it that way, Mr. Carroll. Because sometimes scouts get to enjoying themselves so much here, that they forget what's in the handbook.

These things go by rules, you know. I like Gilbert and I wouldn't want him to get any crazy notions from what these old timers say. There's some talk among the boys — — "

"I think the little fellow's responsible for that," Mr. Carroll laughed. "Gilbert is level-headed and sensible."

"You bet," said Tom. "Well, then, it's all right, and there won't be any broken hearts. I've seen more broken hearts here at camp than broken heads ... You're a new troop, aren't you?" he queried.

"Oh, yes, we haven't got our eyes open yet."

"Goliath seems to have his mouth open for business."

"Yes," Mr. Carroll laughed. "Shall we stroll down to supper?"

"I've got one more call to make if you'll excuse me," said Tom.

"Come up again, won't you?"

"Oh, yes, I make inspection every day. You'll be sick of the sight of me."

He was off again, striding down the little hill. He passed among the tents, around Visitors' Bungalow, and toward the cabins in Good Turn Grove. Somewhat removed from these (a couple of good turns from them, as Roy Blakeley said) was the cabin of Mr. Denny's troop.

The boys were getting ready to go down and they greeted Tom cheerily.

"Where's Hervey?" he asked.

He had not seen Hervey since late the previous night, just after returning from the mountain. Hervey was then so exhausted as hardly to know him. The young assistant fancied a sort of constraint among the boys and he thought that maybe Hervey's condition had taken an alarming turn.

"Ask Mr. D.," said one of the scouts.

"H'lo, Mr. Denny," said Tom, stepping into one of the cabins. No one was there but the scoutmaster. "Where's our wandering boy to-night?"

"He has been dismissed from camp, I'm sorry to say," said Mr. Denny. "Sit down, won't you?"

Tom could hardly speak for astonishment.

"You mean the camp — down at the office — —"

"Oh, no, I sent him home. It was just between him and myself."

"Oh, I see," said Tom, a trifle relieved, apparently. "It wasn't on account of his hurt?"

"Oh, no, he's all right. He just disobeyed me, that's all. That sort of thing couldn't go on, you know. It was getting worse."

Mr. Denny had now had a chance to review his conduct and he found it in all ways justified. He was glad that he had not weakened. Moreover, there was fresh evidence.

"Only just now," he said, "one of the scoutmasters came to me with a notice from the bulletin board utterly ruined by a tomato which Hervey threw. He was greatly annoyed."

"Sure," said Tom.

"I don't exactly blame you, Slade — —"

"Me?"

"But you took Hervey with you across the lake. He had promised me not to leave camp. Where he went, I don't know — —"

"You don't?"

"No, and I don't care. He was picked up by the people in the bus, and if it hadn't been for that I suppose I'd be answerable to his parents for his death. He was very insolent to me."

"He didn't say — —"

"Oh, no, he didn't say anything. He assumed an air of boyish independence; I don't know that I hold that against him."

"But he didn't tell you where he had been—or anything?"

"Why, no. I had no desire to hear that. His fault was in starting. It made no difference where he went."

"Oh."

For a few seconds Tom said nothing, only drummed with his fingers on the edge of the cot on which he sat.

"This is a big surprise to me," he finally said.

"It is a very regrettable circumstance to me," said Mr. Denny.

There ensued a few seconds more of silence. The boys outside could be heard starting for supper.

Tom was the first to speak. "Of course you won't think I'm trying to butt in, Mr. Denny, but there's a rule that the camp can call on all its people in an emergency. The first year the camp opened we had a bad fire here and every kid in the place was set to work. After that they made a rule. Sometimes things have to be done in a hurry. I took Hervey and a couple of others across the lake, because I knew something serious had happened over there. I think I had a right to do that. But there's something else. Hervey didn't tell you everything. You said you didn't want him to."

"He has never told me everything. I had always been in the dark concerning him. This tomato throwing makes me rather ashamed, too."

"Yes," said Tom, "that's bad. But will you listen to me if I tell you the whole of that story—the whole business? I've been away from camp all day. I only got here fifteen minutes ago. I know Hervey's a queer kid—hard to understand. I don't know why he didn't speak out——"

"Why, it was because I told him it wouldn't make any difference," said Mr. Denny, a bit nettled. "The important point was known to me and that was that he disobeyed me. I don't think we can gain anything by talking this over, Slade."

"Then you won't listen to me, Mr. Denny?"

"I don't think it would be any use."

Tom paused a moment. He was just a bit nettled, too. Then he stood. And then, just in that brief interval, his lips tightened and his mouth looked just as it used to look in the old hoodlum days—rugged, strong. The one saving, hopeful feature which Mr. Ellsworth, his old scoutmaster, had banked upon then in that sooty, unkempt countenance. They were the lips of a bulldog:

"All right, Mr. Denny," he said respectfully.

CHAPTER XXII

ACTION

Tom strode down to the messboards which, in pleasant weather, were out under the trees. He seemed not at all angry; there was a kind of breezy assurance in his stride and manner. As he reached the messboards where some of the scouts were already seated on the long benches, several noticed this buoyancy in his demeanor.

"H'lo, kiddo," he said to Pee-wee Harris as he passed and ruffled that young gourmand's hair.

Reaching Mr. Carroll, he asked in a cheery undertone, "May I use one of your scouts for a little while?"

"I'll have the whole troop wrapped up and delivered to you," said Mr. Carroll.

"Thanks."

Reaching Gilbert Tyson, he laid his hand on Gilbert's shoulder and whispered to him in a pleasant, offhand way, "Get through and come in the office, I want to speak to you."

In the office, Tom seated himself at one of the resident trustees' desks, spilled the contents of a pigeon hole in hauling out a sheet of the camp stationery, shook his fountain pen with a blithe air of crisp decision and wrote:

To Hervey Willetts, Scout: —

You are hereby required to present yourself before the resident Court of Honor at Temple Camp, which sits in the main pavilion on Saturday, August the second, at ten A. M., and which will at that time hear testimony and decide on your fitness for the Scout Gold Cross award for supreme heroism.

By order of the

RESIDENT COUNCIL.

Pushing back his chair, he strode over to Council Shack, adjoining.

"Put your sig on that, Mr. Collins," said he.

He reëntered the office just as Gilbert Tyson, wearing a look of astonishment and inquiry, and finishing a slice of bread and butter, entered by the other door.

"Tyson," said Tom, as he put the missive in an envelope, "I understand you're a hero, woke up and found yourself famous and all that kind of stuff. Can you sprint? Good. I'm going to give you the chance of your life, and no war tax. Hervey Willetts started for home about three quarters of an hour ago. Never mind why. Deliver this letter to him."

"Where is he?" Gilbert asked.

"I haven't the slightest idea."

"Started for the train, you mean?"

"Now, Tyson, I don't know any more about it than just that—he started for home. To-day's Thursday. He must be here Saturday. Now don't waste time. Here's the letter. Now get out!"

"Just one second," said Gilbert. "How do you know he started for home?"

"How do I know it?" Tom shot back, impatiently.

"Do you think a fellow like Willetts would go home? I'll deliver the letter wherever he is. But he isn't on his way home. I know him."

"Tyson," said Tom, "you're a crackerjack scout. Now get out of here before I throw you out."

CHAPTER XXIII

THE MONSTER

It is better to know your man than to know his tracks. Gilbert Tyson had somehow come to understand Hervey in that one day since his arrival at camp, and he had no intention of exhausting his breath in a futile chase along the road. There, indeed, was a scout for you. He was on the job before he had started.

The road ran behind the camp, the camp lying between the road and the lake. To go to Catskill Landing one must go by this road. Also to make a short cut to Jonesville (where the night express stopped) one must go for the first mile or so along this road. The road was a state road and of macadam, and did not show footprints.

Tyson did not know a great deal about tracking, but he knew something of human nature, he had heard something of Hervey, and he eliminated the road. He believed that he would not overtake Hervey there.

Across the road, at intervals, several trails led up into the thicker woods. One led to the Morton farm, another to Witches' Pond.

Tyson, being new at camp, did not know the direction of these trails, but he knew that all trails go somewhere. He had heard, during the day, that Hervey was on cordial terms with every farmer, squatter, tollgate keeper, bridge tender, hobo, and traveling show for miles around.

So he examined these trails carefully at their beginnings beside the road. Only one of them interested him. Upon this, about ten feet in from the road, was a rectangular area impressed in the earth which, in the woods, was still damp after the storm. With his flashlight Gilbert examined this. He thought a box might have stood there. Then he noticed two ruffled places in the earth, each on one of the long sides of the rectangle. He knew then what it meant; a suit-case had stood there.

If he had known more about the circumstance of Hervey's leaving, he might have been touched by the picture of the wandering minstrel pausing to rest upon his burden, there at the edge of the woods.

So this was the trail. Elated, Gilbert hurried on, pausing occasionally to verify his conviction by a footprint in the caked earth. The consistency of the earth was ideal for footprints. Yes, some one had passed here not more than an hour before. Here and there was an occasional hole in the earth where a stick might have been pressed in, showing that the stormy petrel had sometimes used his stick as a cane.

For half an hour Gilbert followed this trail with a feeling of elation, of triumph. Soon he must overtake the wanderer. After a little, the trail became indistinct where it passed through a low, marshy area. The drenching of the woods by the late storm was apparent still in the low places.

Gilbert trudged through this spongy support, all but losing his balance occasionally. Soon he saw something black ahead of him. This was Witches' Pond, though he did not know it by that name.

As he approached, the ground became more and more spongy and uncertain. It was apparent that the pond had usurped much of the surrounding marsh in the recent rainy spell.

Gilbert had to proceed with caution. Once his leg sank to the knee in the oozy undergrowth. He was just considering whether he had not better abandon a trail which was indeed no longer a trail at all, and pick his way around the pond, when he noticed something a little distance ahead of him which caused him to pause and strain his eyes to see it better in the gathering dusk. As he looked a cold shudder went through him. What he saw was, perhaps, fifty feet off. A log was there, one end of which was in the ground, the other end projecting at an angle. Its position suggested the pictures of torpedoed liners going down, and there passed through Gilbert's agitated mind, all in a flash, a vision of the great Lusitania sinking — slowly sinking.

For this great log was going down. Slowly, very slowly; but it was going down. Or else Gilbert's eyes and the deepening shadows were playing a strange trick....

He dragged his own foot out of the treacherous ground and looked about for safer support. There was a suction as he dragged his foot up which sent his heart to his mouth. "Quicksand," he muttered, shudderingly.

Was it too late? He backed cautiously out of the jaws of this horrible monster of treachery and awful death, feeling his way with each tentative, cautious step. He stood ankle deep, breathing more easily. He was back at the edge of that oozy, clinging, all devouring trap. He breathed easier.

He looked at the log. It was going down. It stood almost upright now, and offering no resistance with its bulk, was sinking rapidly. In a minute it looked like a stump. It shortened. Gilbert stood motionless and watched it, fascinated. Instinctively he retreated a few feet, to still more solid support. He was standing in ordinary mud now.

Down, down....

A long legged bird came swooping through the dusk across the pond, lit upon the sinking trunk, and then was off again.

"Lucky it has wings," Gilbert said. There was no other way to safety.

Down, down, down—it was just a hubble. The oozy mass sucked it in, closed over it. It was gone.

There was nothing but the dusk and the pond, and the discordant croaking of frogs.

Then, close to where the log had been, Gilbert saw something else. It was a little dab of yellow. It grew smaller; disappeared. There was nothing to be seen now but a little spot of gray; probably some swamp growth ...

No....

Just then Gilbert saw upon it a tiny speck which sparkled. There were other specks. He strained his eyes to pierce the growing darkness. He was doubtful, then certain, then doubtful. He advanced, ever so cautiously, a step or two, to see it better.

Yes. It was.

Utterly sick at heart he turned his head away. There before him, still defying by its lightness of weight, the hungry jaws of the heartless, terrible, devouring monster that eats its prey alive, stood the little rimless, perforated and decorated cap of Hervey Willetts. Joyous and buoyant it seemed, defying its inevitable fate with the blithe spirit of its late owner. It floated still, after the log and the suit-case had gone down.

And that was all that was left of the wandering minstrel.

CHAPTER XXIV

GILBERT'S DISCOVERY

Gilbert Tyson was a scout and he could face the worst. He soon got control of himself and began considering what he had better do.

He could not advance one more step without danger. Yet he could not think of going back to camp, with nothing but the report of something he had seen from a distance. He had done nothing. Yet what could he do?

He was at a loss to know how Hervey could have advanced so far into that treacherous mire.

He must have picked his way here and there, knee deep, waist deep, like the reckless youngster he was, until he plunged all unaware into the fatal spot. The very thought of it made Gilbert shudder. Had he called for help? Gilbert wondered. How dreadful it must have been to call for help in those minutes of sinking, and to hear nothing but some mocking echo. What had the victim thought of, while going down — down?

Good scout that he was, Gilbert would not go back to camp without rescuing that one remaining proof of Hervey's tragic end. At least he would take back all that there was to take back.

He pulled out of his pocket a fishline wound on a stick. At the end of the line where a hook was, he fastened several more hooks an inch or two apart. The sinker was not heavy enough for his purpose so he fastened a stone to the end of the line.

As he made these preparations, the rather grewsome thought occurred to him of what he should do and how he would feel if Hervey's head were visible when he pulled the cap away. It caused him to hesitate, just for a few seconds, to make an effort to recover it. Suppose that hat were still on the smothered victim's head....

With his first throw, the stone landed short of the mark and he dragged back a mass of dripping marsh growth, caught by the fish-hooks. His second attempt landed the stone a yard or so beyond the hat and the treacherous character of the ground there was shown by the almost instant submergence of the missile. It was with difficulty that Gilbert dragged it out, and with every pull he feared the cord would snap. But as he pulled, the hat came also. The line was directly across it and the hooks caught it nicely. There was no vestige of any solid object where the cap had been. Gilbert wondered how deep the log had sunk, and the suit-case and—the other....

He shook the clinging mud and marsh growth from the hat and looked at it. He had seen Hervey only twice; once lying unconscious in the bus, and once that very day, when the young wanderer had started off to visit his friend, the farmer. But this cap very vividly and very pathetically suggested its owner. The holes in it were of every shape and size. The buttons besought the beholder to vote for suffrage, to buy liberty bonds, to join the Red Cross, to eat at Jim's Lunch Room, to use only Tylers' fresh cocoanut bars, to give a thought to Ireland. There was a Camp-fire Girls' badge, a Harding pin, a Cox pin, a Debs pin ... Hervey had been non-partisan with a vengeance.

With this cap, the one touching memento of the winner of the Gold Cross, Gilbert started sorrowfully back to camp. The dreadful manner of Hervey's death agitated him and weakened his nerve as the discovery of a body would not have done. There was no provision in the handbook for this kind of a discovery; no face to cover gently with his scout scarf, no arms to lay in seemly posture. One who had been, was not. His death and burial were one. Gilbert could not fit this horrible thought to his mind. It was out of all human experience. He could not rid himself of the ghastly thought of how far down those—those things—had gone.

Slowly he retraced his steps along the trail—thinking. He had read of hats being found floating in lakes, indubitable evidence of drowning, and he had known the owners of these hats to show up at the ends of the stories. But this....

He thought of the alighting of that bird upon the sinking end of the log. How free and independent that bird! How easy its escape. How impossible the escape of any mortal. To carelessly pause upon a log that was going down in quicksand and then to fly away. There was blitheness in the face of danger for you!

Gilbert took his way along the trail, sick at heart. How could he tell Tom Slade of this frightful thing? It was his first day at camp and it would cast a shadow on his whole vacation. Soon he espied a light shining in the distance. That was a camp, no doubt. By leaving the trail and following the light, he could shorten his journey. He was not so sure that he wanted to shorten his journey, but he was ashamed of this hesitancy to face things, so he abandoned the trail and took the light for his guide.

Soon there appeared another light near the first one, and then he knew that he was saving distance and heading straight for camp. He had supposed that the trail went pretty straight from the vicinity of camp to that dismal pond in the woods. But you can never see the whole of a trail at once and it must have formed a somewhat rambling course.

Anyway there were the lights of camp off to the west of the path, and Gilbert Tyson hurried thither.

CHAPTER XXV

A VOICE IN THE DARK

Gilbert soon discovered his mistake. When a trail has brought you to a spot it is best to trust that trail to take you back again. Beacons, artificial beacons, are fickle things. Gilbert had much to learn.

He had lost the trail and he soon found that he was following a phantom. One of the lights was no light at all, but a reflection in a puddle in the woods. The woods were still full of puddles; though the ground was firm it still bore these traces of its recent soaking. And the damage caused by the high wind was apparent on every hand, in fallen trees and broken limbs. There was a pungent odor to the drenched woods.

Gilbert picked his way around these impediments of wetness and débris. The night was clear. There were a few stars but no moon. Doubtless, he thought, the reflection in the puddle was the reflection of a star. Presently he saw something black before him. In his maneuvers to keep to dry ground he had in fact already gone beyond it, and looked back at it, so to say.

Now he could see that the reflection in the puddle was derived from a light on the further side of the black mass. Other little intervening puddles were touched with a faint, shimmering brightness.

Gilbert approached the dark object and saw that it was a fallen tree. The wound in the earth caused by its torn-up roots formed a sort of cavern where the slenderer tentacles hung limp like tropical foliage. If there was a means of entrance to this dank little shelter it must be from the farther side. Even where Gilbert stood the atmosphere was redolent of the damp earth of this crazy little retreat. For retreat it certainly was, because there was a light in it. Gilbert could only see the reflection of the light but he knew whence that reflection was derived.

He approached a little closer and was sure he heard voices. He paused, then advanced a little closer still. Doubtless this freakish little shelter left by the storm was occupied by a couple of hoboes, perhaps thieves.

But Gilbert had played his card and lost. He had forsaken the trail for a light, and the light had not guided him to camp. He doubted if he could find his way to camp from here. You are to remember that Gilbert was a good scout, but a new one.

He approached a little closer, and now he could distinctly hear a voice. Not the voice of a hobo, surely, for it was carolling a blithe song to the listening heavens. Gilbert bent his ear to listen:

Oh, the life of a scout is free,

is free;

He's happy as happy can be,

can be.

He dresses so neat,

With no shoes on his feet;

The life of a scout is free!

The life of a scout is bold,

so bold;

His adventures have never been told,

been told.

His legs they are bare,

And he won't take a dare,

The life of a scout is bold!

The savage gorilla is mild,

is mild;

Compared to the boy scout so wild,

so wild.

He don't go to bed,

And he stands on his head,

The life of a scout is wild!

Gilbert stood petrified with astonishment. In all his excursions through the scout handbook he had never encountered any such formula for scouting as this. No scout hero in Boys' Life had ever consecrated himself to such a program.

There was a pause within, during which Gilbert crept a little closer. He hardly knew any of the boys in camp yet, and the strange voice meant nothing to him. He knew that no member of his troop was there.

"Want to hear another?" the singer asked.

"Shoot," was the laconic reply.

"This one was writ, wrot, wrote for the Camp-fire Girls around the blazing oil stove.

"If I had nine lives like an old tom cat,

I'd chuck eight of them away.

For the more the weight, the less the speed,

And scouts don't carry any more than they need;

And I'd keep just one for a rainy day.

"Good? Want to hear more? Second verse by special request. They're off:

"If I could turn like an old windmill,

I'd do good turns all day;

With noble deeds the day I'd fill.

But you see I'm not an old windmill.

And I ain't just built that way,

I ain't."

Gilbert decided that however unusual were these ballads of scouting, they did not emanate from thief or hobo; and he climbed resolutely over the log. Even the comparative mildness of the savage gorilla to this new kind of scout did not deter him.

The scout anthem continued.

"If I was a roaring old camp-fire,

You bet that I'd go out;

Oh, I'd go out and far and near,

For a camp-fire has the right idea;

And knows what it's about!"

Gilbert crept along the farther side of the log till he came to an opening among the tangled roots. It was a very small but cozy little cave that he found himself looking into. In a general way, it suggested a wicker basket or a cage, except that it was black and damp. Within was a little fire of twigs. Tending it was a young fellow of perhaps twenty years of age, wearing a plaid cap. He was stooping over the little fire. Nearby, in a sort of swing made by binding two hanging tentacles of root, sat the wandering minstrel, swinging his legs to keep his makeshift hammock in motion.

Gilbert Tyson contemplated him in speechless consternation. There he was, the ideal ragged vagabond, and he did not cease swinging even when he discovered the visitor.

"H'lo," he said; "gimme my hat, that's just what I wanted; glad to see you."

Dumbfounded, Gilbert tossed the hat over to him.

"I wouldn't sell that hat," said Hervey, putting it on, "not for a couple of cups of cup custard. Sit down. Here's the chorus.

"Then hurrah for the cat with its nine little lives,

And the good turn windmill, too.

And hurrah for the fire that likes to go out,

When the hour is late like a regular scout;

For that's what I like to do,

I do.

You bet your life I do!"

CHAPTER XXVI

LOVE ME, LOVE MY DOG

"Where did you find the hat?" Hervey inquired. "I bet you can't sit on this without holding on. Were you in the swamp? This is my friend, Mr. Hood—Robin Hood—sometimes I call him Lid instead of Hood. Call him cap if you want to, he doesn't care," he added, still swinging.

Mr. Robin Hood did not seem as much at ease as his young companion. He seemed rather troubled and glanced sideways at Gilbert.

"We should worry about his name if he doesn't want to give it, hey?" Hervey said, winking at Gilbert. "What's in a name?"

Gilbert was shrewd enough not to mention Tom but to give his visit the dignity of highest authority.

"Well, this is a big surprise to me," he said, "and I'm mighty glad it's this way," he added with a deep note of sincerity and relief in his voice. "I was sent from the office to find you and give you this note. I tracked you to the pond and I thought—golly, I'm glad it isn't so—but I thought you went down in the quicksand. I near got into it myself."

"Me?"

"Yes, how did you— —"

"Easiest thing in the world. I knew if I could get to the log—did you see the log?"

"It isn't there now."

"I knew if I could get to that I could jump from it to the pond."

"And did you?"

"Surest thing. I kept chucking the suit-case ahead and stepping on it. I had an old board, too. I guess they're both gone down by now."

"Yes."

"When I got to the log I was all hunk—for half a minute. 'One to get ready,' that's what I said. Oh, boy, going down. Toys and stationery in the basement."

Just in that moment Gilbert thought of the bird.

"Yes?" he urged, "and then?"

"One to get ready,

One to jump high,

One to light in the pond or die."

"And you did it? I heard you were reckless. Here, read the note," Gilbert said with unconcealed admiration. The wandering minstrel had made another capture.

He was, however, a little sobered as he opened the envelope. He had never been the subject of an official missive before. He had never been honored by a courier. He had won badges and had an unique reputation for stunts. But when the momentary sting had passed it cannot be said that he left camp with any fond regrets. On the other hand, he bore the camp and his scoutmaster no malice now. He who forgets orders may also forget grievances. In Hervey's blithe nature there was no room for abiding malice.

"What are they trying to hand me now?" he asked, reading the notice.

"I don't know anything about it," said Gilbert; "I think you have to come back, don't you?"

"Sure, I've got the Gold Cross wished on me."

"The cross?" said Gilbert in admiring surprise. "What for?"

"Search me. They're going to test some money or something—testimony, that's it. Something big is going to happen in my young life."

"You'll go back?" Gilbert asked anxiously.

"Sure, if Robin Hood can go with me. Love me, love my dog."

"I don't want to go there," said the young fellow; "you kids better go."

"Then that's the end of the red cross," said Hervey, still swinging. "I mean the Gold Cross or the double cross or whatever you call it. What'd'you say, Hoody? They have good eats there. Will you come and see me cop the cross?"

"He just happened to blow in here," said the stranger, by way of explaining Hervey's presence to Gilbert. "I was knocking around in the woods and bunking in here."

Gilbert was a little puzzled, but he did not ask any questions. He was thoughtful and tactful. He had a pretty good line on Hervey's nature, too.

"Of course, Hervey has to go back," he said, as much for Hervey's benefit as for the stranger's. "I say all three of us go. You'll like to see the camp— —"

"They've got a washed-out cove and an oven for making marshmallows, and a scoutmasters' meeting-place with a drain-pipe you can climb up to the roof on, 'n everything," said Hervey in a spirit of fairness toward the camp and its attractions. "They've got messboards you can do hand-springs on when the cook isn't around. I bet you can't do the double flop, Hoody."

"Well, then, we'll all go?" Gilbert asked rather anxiously.

Hervey spread out his arms by way of saying that anything that suited Gilbert and the stranger would suit him.

So the three started off to camp, the stranger rather hesitating, Gilbert highly elated with his success, and Hervey perfectly agreeable to anything which meant action.

It was characteristic of Hervey that he really had not the faintest idea of why he was to be honored with the highest scout award. He had apparently forgotten all about his almost superhuman exploit. He would never have mentioned it nor thought of it. He did recall it in that moment of humiliation when Mr. Denny had talked with him. But he would not speak of it even then. He would suffer disgrace first. And how much less was he likely to think of it now! Surely the Gold Cross had nothing to do with that fiasco which had ended in unconsciousness. That was not supreme heroism. There was something wrong, somewhere. That was just a stunt....

Well, he would take things as they came—quicksand, a frantic run in storm and darkness, new friends, the Gold Cross, anything....

Was there one soul in all that great camp that really understood him?

As they picked their way through the woods, following his lead (for he alone knew the way) he edified them with another song, for these ballads which had made him the wandering minstrel he remembered even if he remembered nothing else.

"You wouldn't think to look at me

That I'm as good as good can be—

a little saint.

You wouldn't care to make a bet,

That I'm the teacher's little pet—

I ain't."

CHAPTER XXVII

TOM LEARNS SOMETHING

Tom's absence through the day had resulted in an accumulation of work upon his table. His duties were chiefly active but partly clerical. After supper he started to clear away these matters.

The camp had already been in communication with Mr. Temple, its founder, and plans had been made for an inspection of the washed-out cove by engineers from the city. It was purposed to build a substantial dam at that lowest and weakest place on the lake shore. There was a memorandum asking Tom to be prepared to show these men the fatal spot on the following morning.

Matters connected with the meeting of the resident Court of Honor next day had also to be attended to. Several dreamers of high awards would have a sleepless night in anticipation of that meeting. Hervey Willetts would probably sleep peacefully — if he went to bed at all.

It was half an hour or so before Tom got around to looking over the names of new arrivals. These were card indexed by the camp clerk, and Tom always looked the cards over in a kind of casual quest of familiar names, and also with the purpose of getting a line on first season troops. It was his habit to make prompt acquaintance with these and help them over the first hard day or so of strangeness.

In glancing over these names, he was greatly astonished to find on the list of Mr. Carroll's troop, the name of William Corbett. The identity of this name with that of the victim of the automobile accident greatly interested him, and he recalled then for the first time, that this troop had come from Hillsburgh, in the vicinity of which the accident had occurred. Yet, according to the newspaper, the victim of the accident had been killed, or mortally injured.

As Tom pondered on this coincidence of names there ran through his mind one of those snatches of song which Hervey Willetts was fond of singing:

Some boys were killed and some were not,

Of those that went to war;

And a lot of boys are dying now,

That never died before.

Before camp-fire was started Tom hunted up Mr. Carroll.

"I see you have a William Corbett in your troop, Mr. Carroll," said he.

"Oh, yes, that's Goliath."

"He — he wasn't the kid who was knocked down by an auto?"

"Why, yes, he was. You know about that?"

Tom hesitated. The newspapers had not yet had time to publish the sensational accounts of Harlowe's tragic death on the mountain and the facts about this harrowing business had not been made public in camp.

"I thought the kid was killed," Tom said.

"Oh, no, that was just newspaper talk. It's a long way from being mortally injured in a newspaper to being killed, Mr. Slade."

"Y-es, I dare say you're right," said Tom, still astonished.

"Yes, the little codger has a weak heart," said Mr. Carroll. "When the machine struck him it knocked him down and he was picked up unconscious. Probably he looked dead as he lay there. I dare say that's what frightened the man in the machine. No, it was just his heart," he added. "A couple of the boys in my troop knew the family, mother did washing for them or something of that sort, and so we got in touch with the little codger and there was our good turn all cut out for us.

"You know, Slade, we have a kind of an institution — troop good turn. Ever hear of anything like that? So we brought him along. He's a kind of a scout in the chrysalis stage. He doesn't even know what happened to him. A good part of his life has been spent in hospitals; he'll pick up though. I think the newspaper reporters did more harm than the autoist. Do you know, Slade, I think the man may have just got panicky, like some of the soldiers in the war."

"I've seen a fellow shrink like a whipped cur at the sound of a cannon and then I've seen him flying after the enemy like a fiend," said Tom.

"Yes, human nature's a funny thing," said Mr. Carroll.

Tom's mind was divided between admiration of this kind, tolerant, generous scoutmaster and astonishment at what he had learned.

"Well, that's news to me," he said.

"Yes, the main thing is to build the little codger up now," Mr. Carroll mused aloud.

"Mr. Carroll," said Tom, "Gilbert didn't say anything about going up the mountain with me last night?"

"N-no, I don't know that he did."

"The trustees didn't want anything said about the matter here in camp, or the whole outfit would be going up the mountain. But I suppose the papers will have the whole business by to-morrow, and you might as well have it now. The fellow who ran down the kid was found crushed to death on the mountain last night. His name was Aaron Harlowe."

Tom told the whole harrowing episode to Mr. Carroll, who listened with interest, commenting now and again upon the tragic sequel of the auto accident. It was plain, throughout, however, that his chief interest was in his little charge, Goliath.

"That's a very strange thing," he said; "it has a smack of Divine justice about it, if one cares to look at it that way. Have you any theory of just how it happened?"

"I haven't got any time for theories, Mr. Carroll; not with four new troops coming to-morrow. It's a closed book now, I suppose. There are some funny things about the whole business. But one thing sure, the man's dead. I have a hunch he got crazed and rattled and hid here and there and was afraid they'd catch him and finally went up the mountain. He thought he had killed the kid, you see. I'd like to know what went on inside his head, wouldn't you?"

"Yes, I would."

Several of Mr. Carroll's troop, seeing him talking with Tom, approached and hung about as this chat ended. Wherever Tom Slade was, scouts were attracted to that spot as flies are attracted to sugar. They stood about, listening, and staring at the young camp assistant.

"Well, how do you think you like us up here?" Tom asked, turning abruptly from his talk with their scoutmaster. "Think you're going to have a good time?"

"You said something," one piped up.

"Where's Gilbert?" another asked.

"Oh, he'll be back in a little while," Tom said. "I sent him on an errand and I suppose he got lost."

"He did not!" several vociferated.

"No?" Tom smiled.

"You bet he didn't!"

"Well," said Tom, laughing, "if you fellows want to get into the mix-up, keep your eyes on the bulletin board. Everything is posted there, hikes and things. You'll like most of the things you see there."

"I'm crazy about tomatoes," one of the scouts ventured.

Tom smiled at Mr. Carroll and Mr. Carroll smiled at Tom.

There seemed to be a sort of unspoken agreement among them all that Hervey Willetts should be thought of ruefully, and in a way of disapproval. But, oddly enough, none of them seemed quite able to conceal a sneaking liking for him, shown rather than expressed.

And there you have an illustration of Hervey's status in camp....

CHAPTER XXVIII

THE BLACK SHEEP

The scouts were all around the camp-fire when Gilbert Tyson returned with his captives. As they crossed the road and came upon the camp grounds, the stranger seemed apprehensive and ill at ease, but Hervey with an air of sweeping authority informed him that everything was all right, that he would fix it for him.

"Don't you worry," he said; "I know all the high mucks here. You leave it to me." He was singularly confident for one in disgrace. "I'll get you a job, all right. When you see Slady or Uncle Jeb you just tell them you're a friend of mine." Robin Hood seemed somewhat reassured by the words of one so influential. By way of giving him a cheery reminder of certain undesirable facts and reconciling him to a life of toil, Hervey sang as they made their way to the office.

"You gotta go to work,

You gotta go to work,

You gotta go to work—

That's true.

And the reason why you gotta go to work

IS

The work won't come to you

SEE?

"I gotta go to bed,

I gotta go to bed,

Like a good little scout—

You see.

And the reason why I gotta go to bed

IS

The bed won't come to me.

D'you see?

The bed won't come to me."

This ballad of toil and duty (which were Hervey's favorite themes) was accompanied by raps on Gilbert's head with a stick, which became more and more vigorous as they approached the office. Here the atmosphere of officialdom did somewhat subdue the returning prodigal son and he removed his precious hat as they entered.

This matter was in Tom Slade's hands and he was going to see it through alone. From camp-fire his watchful eye had seen the trio passing through the grove and he was in the office before they reached it.

The office was a dreadful place, where the mighty John Temple himself held sway on his occasional visits, where councilmen and scoutmasters conferred, and where there was a bronze statue of Daniel Boone. Hervey had many times longed to decorate the sturdy face of the old pioneer with a mustache and whiskers, using a piece of trail-sign chalk.

At present he was seized by a feeling of respectful diffidence, and stood hat in hand, a trifle uncomfortable. Robin Hood was uncomfortable too, but he was in for it now. He was relieved to see that the official who confronted him was an easy-going offhand young fellow of about his own age, dressed in extreme negligée, sleeves rolled up, shirt open, face and throat brown like the brown of autumn. It seemed to make things easier for the trio that Tom vaulted up onto the bookkeeper's high desk, as if he were vaulting a fence, and sat there swinging his legs, the very embodiment of genial companionship.

"Well, Gilbert, you got away with it, huh?"

"Here he is," said Gilbert proudly. "I found him in a kind of cave in the woods — — "

"Gilbert deserves all the credit for finding me," Hervey interrupted. "You've got to hand it to him, I'll say that much."

"It isn't everybody who can find you, is it?" said Tom.

"Believe me, you said something," Hervey ejaculated.

"Well, I'm going to say some more," Tom laughed.

"This is my friend," said Hervey; "Robin Hood, but I don't know his real name. He's a good friend of mine, and he can play the banjo only he hasn't got one with him, and I want to get him a job."

"Any friend of yours — —" Tom began and winked at Gilbert.

"What did I tell you?" said Hervey. "Didn't I tell you I'd fix it?"

"I'm glad to meet you, Mr. Hood," said Tom. "We're expecting to be pretty busy here, I can say that much," he added cautiously.

"I was just roaming the woods," said the stranger. "I haven't got any home; out of luck. The boys insisted on my coming."

"Strangers always welcome," said Tom cheerily.

It was, indeed, true that strangers were always welcome. Temple Camp was down on the hobo's blue book as a hospitable refuge. Stranded show people had known its sheltering kindness. Moreover, Tom was not likely to make particular inquiry about Hervey's chance acquaintances. The wandering minstrel had brought in laid-off farm hands, a strolling organ grinder with a monkey, not to mention two gypsies, a peddler of rugs and other strays.

"Well, Tyson," said Tom, clasping his hands behind his head and swinging his legs in a way of utmost good humor, "suppose you take Mr. Hood over to camp-fire and see if he can stand for some of those yarns. Tell Uncle Jeb he's going to hang around till morning. You stay here, Hervey. I'd like to hear about your adventures. Let's see, how many lives have you got left now?"

"Believe me, I did some stunt," said Hervey.

CHAPTER XXIX

STUNTS AND STUNTS

For a minute or two, Tom sat swinging his legs, contemplating Hervey.

"When it comes to stunts," said he, "you're down and out. You belong to the 'also rans.'"

"Me?"

"Yes, you."

"I can— —"

"Oh, yes, you can do a lot. You ought to join the Camp-fire Girls. You were asked to stay at camp—I'm not talking about yesterday. I'm talking about all summer. There's an easy stunt. But you fell down on it. Don't talk to me about stunts."

"Do you think it's easy to hang around camp all the time? It's hard, you can bet."

"Sure, it's a stunt. And you can't do it. Little Pee-wee Harris can do it, but you can't. Don't talk stunts to me. I know what a stunt is."

"What's a stunt?" Hervey asked, trying to conceal the weakness of his attitude with a fine air of defiance.

"Why, a stunt is something that is hard to do, that's all."

"You tell me— —"

"I'll tell you something I want you to do and you're afraid to do it—you're afraid."

"I won't take a dare from anybody," Hervey shouted.

"Well, you'll take one from me."

"You dare me to do something and see."

"All righto. I dare you to go up to your troop's cabin after camp-fire and tell Mr. Denny that you've been a blamed nuisance and that you're out to do the biggest stunt you ever did. And that is to do what you're told. Tell him I dared you to do it, and tell him what you said about not taking a dare from anybody. Tell him you never knew about its being a stunt.

"Of course I know you won't do it, because it's hard, and I know you're not game. I just want to show you that you're a punk stunt-puller. I dare you to do it! I DARE you to do it!"

"I won't take a dare from anybody!" said Hervey, excitedly.

"Oh, yes, you will. You'll take one from me. You're a four-flusher, that's what you are. Go ahead. I dare you to do it. You won't take a dare, hey? I double dare you to! There. Now let's see. Go up there and tell Mr. Denny you're going to get away with the biggest thing you ever tried — the biggest stunt. And to-morrow morning before the Court meets you come in here and see Mr. Fuller and Uncle Jeb and me. Now don't ask any questions. You came in here all swelled up, regular fellow and all that sort of thing, and I'm calling your bluff."

"You call me a bluffer?" Hervey shouted.

"The biggest bluffer outside of Pine Bluff."

"Me?"

"Yes, you."

"I wouldn't take a dare from you or anybody like you!"

"Actions speak louder than words."

"I never saw the stunt yet — — "

"Well, here it is right now. I dare you. I dare you," said Tom, jumping down and looking right in Hervey's face, "I DOUBLE DARE YOU!"

Hervey grabbed his hat from the bench.

"A kid that gives a double dare

For shame and grins he must prepare."

he shouted.

"That's me," said Tom.

Before he realized what had happened, he heard the door slam and he found himself alone, laughing. Hervey had departed, in wrath and desperation, bent upon his next stunt.

CHAPTER XXX

THE DOUBLE DARE

Mr. Denny's troop had turned in with the warmth of the roaring camp-fire still lingering in their cheeks when the black sheep went up the hill. The scoutmaster, sitting in his tepee, was writing up the troop's diary in the light of a railroad lantern. He showed no great surprise at his wandering scout's arrival.

"Well, Hervey," said he. "Back again? I told you it would be better to wait till morning. Missed the train, eh? You see my advice is sometimes best after all." He did not look up but continued writing. If Hervey had expected to create a sensation he was disappointed. "Better go to bed and catch the nine fifty-two in the morning," said Mr. Denny kindly.

"I came back because Tom Slade sent for me. I've got to get a medal, but I don't care anything about that."

"So? What's that for?"

"I always said that fellow Slade was a friend of mine, but I wouldn't let him put one over on me, I wouldn't."

"You mean he was just fooling you about the medal?"

"Maybe you can tell," said Hervey. "Because anyway I didn't do anything to win a—the Gold Cross."

Mr. Denny raised his eyebrows in frank surprise. "The Gold Cross?"

"I don't care anything about that, anyway," said Hervey; "but I wouldn't take a dare from anybody; I never did yet."

"No?"

"He said—that fellow said—he said I wouldn't dare to come up here and tell you that I can—do anything I want to do."

"That's just what you've been doing, Hervey."

"But you know I'm good on stunts? And he said—this is just what he said—he said I couldn't do that kind of a stunt—staying here when I'm told to. He dared me to. Would you take a double dare if you were me? They're worse than single ones."

"N-no, I don't know that I would," said Mr. Denny, thoughtfully.

"He said I wouldn't dare—do you know what a four flusher is?"

"Why—y-es."

"He said I wouldn't dare to come up here and tell you that I know I'm wrong to make so much trouble and he said I couldn't do a stunt like staying in camp. Would you let any fellow call you a Camp-fire Girl— would you? Gee Williger, that stunt's a cinch!"

Mr. Denny closed his book, leaving his pen in it as a book-mark, and clasping his hands, listened attentively. It was the first slight sign of surrender. He looked inquiringly and not unkindly at the figure that stood before him in the dim lantern light. He noted the torn clothing, the wrinkled stocking, the outlandish hat with its holes and trinkets. He could see, just see, those clear gray eyes, honest, reckless, brave....

"Yes, Hervey?"

"Of course you don't have to keep me here, I don't mean that. Because that's another thing, anyway. Only I want you to tell Slade that I did dare, because I wouldn't take a double dare not even from—from Mr. Temple, I wouldn't. So then he'll know I'm not afraid of you. Because even you wouldn't say I'm a coward."

"No."

"I can do any stunt going, I'll let him know, and I won't take a double dare from anybody. Because I made a resolution when I was in the third primary grade."

"And you've always kept it?"

"You think I'd bust a resolution? You have bad luck for eight years if you do that."

"I see."

"No, siree!"

"And so you think you could do this stunt?"

"I can do any stunt going. Do you know what I did — — "

"Just a second, Hervey. I'd like to see you get away with that stunt."

"But I'm not asking you to keep me here," Hervey said, giving his stocking a hitch, "because I'm a good loser, I am. But I want you to tell that fellow Slade — I used to think he was a friend of mine — I want you to tell him that I bobbed that dare."

"Bobbed it?"

"Yes, that means put it back on him."

Mr. Denny paused.

"Why don't you tell him yourself, Hervey?"

"Because he doesn't have to believe me."

"Has any one ever accused you of lying, Hervey?"

"Do you think I'd let anybody?"

"Hmm, well, I think you'd better bob that dare yourself. But of course you ought to follow it up with the stunt."

"Oh, sure — only — — "

"I'll give you the chance to do that. My sporting blood is up now — — "

"That's just the way with me," said Hervey; "that's where you and I are alike."

"Yes. I think we'll have to put this fellow Slade where he belongs."

"You leave that to me," said Hervey.

There was a pause of a few moments. The whole camp had turned in by now and distant voices had ceased. A cricket chirped somewhere close by. An acorn fell from a tree overhead and rolled down the roof of the troop cabin a few yards distant, the sound of its falling emphasized by the stillness. Hervey hitched up his stocking again. Mr. Denny watched him. Perhaps he was studying this wandering minstrel of his more closely than ever before. It may have been that the silence and isolation were on Hervey's side....

"Anyway, you don't have to keep me here, because—and I didn't come back for that."

"Hervey, you spoke about a medal—the Gold Cross. You don't mean the supreme heroism award, of course. Slade didn't try to lure you back with hints about such a thing?"

"Hanged if I know what he meant."

"He sent a note after you? Have you it with you?"

"I made paper bullets out of it to shoot at lightning bugs on the way home."

"Did he actually mention the Gold Cross?"

"I think he did—sure I never did anything to win that, you can bet."

"No. And I think Slade adopted very questionable tactics to get you back. Doubtless his intentions were good — —"

"I wouldn't let that fellow ruin my young life—don't worry."

"Well, you'd better turn in now, Hervey, and don't stay awake thinking about dares and stunts and awards."

And indeed Hervey did not stay awake thinking of any such things, especially awards. In more than one tent and cabin on that Friday night were sleepless heads, tossing and visioning the morrow which would bring them merit badges, and perhaps awards of higher honor—silver, bronze....

But the head of Hervey Willetts rested quietly and his sleep was sound. He took things as they came, as he had taken the letter out of Gilbert's hands. There was a mistake somewhere, or else Tom Slade had caught him and brought him back by a mean trick and a false promise. But he did not hold that against Tom. What he held against Tom was that Tom had made him take a double dare. He knew he had done nothing to win so high an honor as that golden treasure, so rare, so coveted.... What he had done was already ancient history and forgotten. And it had no relation to the Gold Cross. And so he slept peacefully.

The thing that he most treasured was his decorated hat, and so that this might not get away from him again, he kept it under his pillow....

CHAPTER XXXI

THE COURT IN SESSION

From his conversation with Tom, Mr. Denny knew (if indeed he had not known it before) that the young assistant had a strong liking for this bah, bah black sheep. He knew that Tom had been responsible for Hervey's latest truancy and he believed that Tom, knowing that a little trick was the only way to bring Hervey back, might have played such a little trick, then sent him up the hill to square himself.

Mr. Denny was quite in sympathy with the stunt and double dare business, but he did not approve of trying to circumvent Hervey by dangling the Gold Cross before his eyes. He was afraid that Hervey would not forget this and that the disappointment would be keen. As we know, Tom was dead set against this kind of thing. Mr. Denny did not know that. But he did know that Hervey was unfamiliar with the rigorous requirements for winning the highest award, for most of the pages in Hervey's handbook had been used to make torches and paper bullets. Mr. Denny was resolved that Tom Slade should not get away with such tactics unrebuked. He was resolved to speak to the Honor Court about it in the morning. He would not have one of his boys made the victim of vain hopes....

Early in the morning, Tom took a little stroll with Robin Hood and improved his acquaintance. Tom liked odd people as much as Hervey did and he found this unfortunate stranger rather interesting. One thing, in particular, he learned from him which was of immediate interest to him and which Hervey, with characteristic heedlessness, had forgotten to mention.

"I dare say we can dig you up something to do," said Tom, "when the work on the dam gets started. That'll be in two or three days, I guess. Suppose you hang around."

"I'd like to stay right here for the rest of the summer," said the young fellow. "I'm out of luck and I'm all in."

"France?" Tom queried. For soldiers out of luck were not uncommon in camp.

"No, just hard luck; lost my grip, that's all."

"Well, hang around and maybe you'll pull together. I've seen lots of shell-shock; had it myself, in fact."

"Oh, it's nothing like that."

"Come in and see the Supreme Court in session, won't you? It's great. We have this twice during the summer. Reminds you of the League of Nations in session.... H'lo, Shorty, what are you here for? More merit badges?"

Outside the main pavilion the choicest spirits of camp were loitering; Pee-wee Harris still working valiantly on the end of his breakfast, Roy Blakeley of the Silver Foxes, Bert Winton on from Ohio with the Bengal Tigers, and Brent Gaylong, leader of the Church Mice from Newburgh. He was a sort of scoutmaster and patrol leader rolled into one, was Brent, a lanky, slow moving fellow with a funny squint to his face, and a quiet way of seeing the funny side of things. You had only to look at him to laugh.

"Tickets purchased from speculators not good," he was saying.

Inside, the place was half filled with scouts, with a sprinkling of scoutmasters. The members of the resident Court of Honor were already seated behind a table and business was going forward. Much had already been despatched.

After a little while Mr. Denny came in and sat down. Other scoutmasters sauntered in, and scouts singly and in groups. One proud scout went out with three new merit badges and was vociferously cheered outside.

Another didn't quite make the pathfinder's badge; another the camp honor flag for good turns. Still another got the Life Scout badge, and so it went. Honor jobs for the ensuing week were given out. There were many strictly camp awards, not found in the handbook. The Temple Paddle was awarded to a proud canoeist. Scouts came and went. Sometimes the interest was keen and sometimes it lagged.

Hervey Willetts came sauntering up from the boat landing, his hat at a rakish angle, and trying to balance an oar-lock on his nose. He had an air of wandering aimlessly so that his arrival at the pavilion seemed quite a matter of chance. A morning song was on his lips:

The life of a scout is sweet,

is sweet,

The rubbish he throws in the street,

the street.

He uses soft words,

And he shoots all the birds;

The life of a scout is sweet.

Being a lone, blithe spirit, a kind of scout skylark as one might say, he had not many friends in camp. The rank and file laughed at him, were amused at his naïve independence, and regarded him, not as a poor scout, but rather as not exactly a scout at all. They did not see enough of him; he flew too high. He was his own best companion.

Consequently when he sauntered with a kind of whimsical assurance into that exalted official conclave most of them thought that he had dropped in as he might have dropped into the lake. There was a little touch of pathos, too, in the fact that the loiterers outside did not speak to him as he passed in. It was just that they did not know him well enough; he was not one of them. He was the oddest of odd numbers, a stormy petrel indeed, and they did not know how to take him.

So he was alone amid three hundred scouts....

CHAPTER XXXII

OVER THE TOP

Tom had waited patiently for Hervey to arrive. His propensity for not arriving had troubled Tom. But whether by chance or otherwise there he was, and Tom lost no time in getting to his feet.

"Before the court closes," he said, "I want to ask to have a blank filled out to be sent to the National Honor Court, on a claim for the Gold Cross award. I would like to get it endorsed by the Local Council to-day so it will get to National Headquarters Monday."

You could have heard a pin drop in that room. The magic words Gold Cross brought every whispering, dallying scout to attention. There was a general rustle of straightening up in seats. The continuous departing ceased. Faces appeared at the open windows.

The Gold Cross.

Mr. Denny looked at Tom. The young assistant, in his usual negligée, was very offhand and thoroughly at ease. He seemed to know what he was talking about. All eyes were upon him.

"If you want the detailed statements of the three witnesses written out, that can be done. But the National Court will take the recommendation without that if it's endorsed by the Local Council. That was done in the case of Albert Nesbit, who won the Gold Cross here three years ago. I'd rather do it that way."

"What is the name, Mr. Slade?"

"Willetts—Hervey Willetts. You spell it with two T's."

"This can be done without witnesses, on examination, Mr. Slade."

"The winner isn't a good subject for examination," said Tom; "I think the witnesses would be better."

"Just so."

"I might say," said Tom, "that this is the first chance I've had to tell about this thing. On the night of the storm I sent Willetts from the cove and told him to catch the bus and stop it before it reached the bridge. I didn't think he could do it but I didn't say so. He had two miles to go through the storm, running all the way. The wind was in his face. Of course we all know what the storm was. His scoutmaster had told him not to leave camp. If this was an emergency then it comes under By-law Twenty-seven. You'll have to decide that. It was on account of the flood I took him, not on account of the bus. The lake was running out."

"Did he reach the bus?" Mr. Fuller asked.

"He reached the bus, but he doesn't know how. The last he remembered is that he fell because his foot was caught in a hole. I don't know, nobody knows how he did that thing. Here's a man who was in the woods that night and saw him. He met him about half way and says he was so exhausted and excited he couldn't speak. He told this man that he had to hurry on to save some people's lives. He meant the people in the bus. How he got from the place where he fell to the bus is a mystery. When he did get there he couldn't speak, so he grabbed one of the horses. His foot was wrenched and he was unconscious.

"When they got him in the bus he muttered something and they thought he was talking about his foot. It was the bridge he was talking about. But what he said prompted Mr. Carroll to send another scout forward, and he stopped the bus. That's all there is to it. He got there and it nearly killed him. Darby Curren, who is here to tell you, thought he was a spook.

"Now these three people, Mr. Hood, Darby Curren and Mr. Carroll, can tell you what they know about it. It's one of those cases where the real facts didn't come out. Hervey Willetts saved the lives of twenty-two people at grave danger to his own. That satisfies the handbook. He doesn't care four cents about the Gold Cross, but right is right, and I'm here to see that he gets it. Stand up, Hervey. Stand out in the aisle." Suddenly Tom was seated.

So there stood the wandering minstrel, alone. Even his champion was not in evidence. Nor was his troop there to share the glory with him. His scoutmaster was there, but he seemed too dazed to speak. And so the stormy petrel stood alone, as he would always stand alone. Because there was no one like him.

"Willetts is the name? Hervey Willetts?"

"I got a middle name, but I don't bother with it."

"What troop?"

And so the cut and dried business, so strange and unattractive to Hervey, of filling in the blank, went on. He did not greatly care for indoor sports. There was a lull in the general interest. Scouts began lounging and whispering again.

In that interval of restlessness, an observant person might have noticed, sitting in the back part of the room, the rather ungainly figure of the tall fellow, Brent Gaylong, organizer of the Church Mice of Newburgh. He seemed to be the center of a clamoring, interested, little group.

Roy Blakeley's brown, crinkly hair could be seen through the gaps made by other heads. Gaylong's knees were up against the back of the seat in front of him, thus forming a sort of slanting desk, on which he held a writing tablet. His head was cocked sideways as if in humorous but stern criticism of his own work. On somebody's suggestion he wrote something then crossed it out. There were evidently too many cooks at the broth, but he was ludicrously patient and considerate, being no doubt chief cook himself. There was something very funny about his calm, preoccupied demeanor amid that clamoring throng. The proceedings in the room interested him not.

Nor did the business interest many others now. There was a continuous drift toward the door and the crowd of loiterers outside increased and became noisy. The wandering minstrel stood alone.

The voice of the chairman droned on, "Hill cabin twenty-two. Right. We will talk with these gentlemen afterwards. It may be a week or two before you get this, Willetts. It has to come from the National Court of Honor. Meanwhile, the Camp thanks you, and is proud of you, for your extraordinary feat of heroism. It's most unusual — —"

"Trust him for that," some one interrupted.

"I could run faster than that if I had sneaks," said Hervey.

"I'm afraid no one would have seen you at all, then," said Mr. Carlson.

"All you've got to do is double your fists and look through them and you can see a mile. It's like opera glasses."

"STAND UP, HERVEY. STAND OUT IN THE AISLE."

Tom Slade's Double Dare.   Page 180

"So? Well, let us shake hands with you, my boy."

The next thing Hervey knew, Mr. Denny's arm was over his shoulder, while with his other hand he was shaking the hand of the young camp assistant.

"That's all right, Mr. Denny," said Tom.

"Slade, I want you to know how much I respect you — —"

"It's all in the day's work, Mr. Denny."

"I want you to know that Hervey appreciates your friendship. You believe he — —"

"I believe he's a wild Indian," Tom laughed. "Or maybe a squirrel, huh? Hey, Hervey? On account of climbing.... You know, Mr. Denny, those are the two things that can't be tamed, an Indian and a squirrel. You can tame a lion, but you can't tame a squirrel."

Mr. Denny listened, smiling, all the while patting Hervey's shoulder.

"Well, after all, who wants to tame a squirrel?" said he.

So these two lingered a few minutes to chat about lions and Indians and squirrels and things. And that was Hervey's chance to get away.

No admiring throng followed him out. His own troop was not there and knew nothing of his triumph. Probably he never thought of these things. A scoutmaster grabbed his hand and said, "Wonderful, my boy!" Hervey smiled and seemed surprised.

Outside they were sitting around on railings and steps and squatting on the grass. There was a little ripple of murmuring as he passed through the sprawling throng, but no one spoke to him. That was not because they did not appreciate, but because he was different and a stranger. Perhaps it was because they did not know just how to take him. He didn't exactly fit in....

His ambling course had taken him perhaps a hundred feet, when he heard some one shout, "Let'er go!"

Before he realized it, his own favorite tune filled the air, they were hurling it straight at him and the voices were loud and clear, though the words were strange.

"Everybody!"

"He's one little bully athlete,

so fleet;

At sprinting he's got us all beat,

yes, beat.

He can climb, he can stalk,

He can win in a walk;

He's a scout from his head to his feet—

THAT'S YOU.

He's a scout from his head to his feet."

He turned and stood stark still. Some of them, in the vehemence of their song, had risen and formed a little compact group. And again they sang the verse, the words THAT'S YOU pouring out of the throat of Pee-wee Harris like a thunderbolt. Hervey blinked. His eyes glistened. Through their haze he could see the lanky figure of the tall fellow, Brent Gaylong, sitting upon the fence, his feet propped up on the lower rail, a pair of shell spectacles half way down his nose, and waving a little stick like the leader of an orchestra. He was very sober and looked absurdly funny.

"Let him have the other one!" some one shouted.

Gaylong rapped upon the fence with his little stick, and then gave it a graceful twirl which was an improvement on Sousa.

The voices rose clear and strong:

"We don't care a rap for the flings he springs;

He doesn't mean half of the things he sings.

We're all down and out

When it comes to a scout

That can run just as if he had wings and things.

That can run just as if he had wings!"

If Hervey had waited as long on the log in the quicksand as he waited now, there would have been no Gold Cross. But he could not move, he stood as one petrified, his eyes glistening. The wandering minstrel had been caught by his own tune.

"Over the top," some one shouted.

He was surrounded.

"That's you! That's you!"

they kept singing. He had never been caught in such a mix-up before. He saw them all crowding about him, saw Roy Blakeley's merry face and the sober face of Brent Gaylong, the spectacles still half way down his nose and the baton over his ear like a lead pencil. They took his hat, tossed it around, and handed it back to him.

"No room on that for the Cross," said Gaylong; "he'll have to pin it on his stocking; combination Gold Cross and garter. Supreme heroism—keeping a stocking up——"

There was no getting out of this predicament. He could escape the quicksand but he couldn't escape this. He looked about as if to consider whether he could make a leap over the throng.

"Watch out or he'll pull a stunt," one shouted.

But there was really no hope for him. The wandering minstrel was caught at last. And the funny part of the whole business was that he was caught by one of his own favorite tunes. The tunes which had caught so many others....

CHAPTER XXXIII
QUESTIONS

Hervey had now no incentive to leave the vicinity of camp. Doubtless he could have performed the great stunt without outside help (now that he knew it to be a stunt) but luck favored him as it usually did, and the new work going forward in the cove was enough to occupy his undivided attention.

He made his headquarters there and hobnobbed with civil engineers and laborers in the true democratic spirit which was his. The consulting engineer they called him, which was odd, because Hervey never consulted anybody about anything. The men all liked him immensely.

Another to benefit by the work on the new dam was Robin Hood, or Mr. Hood as he was respectfully called. He ran the flivver truck between the camp and the cove, carrying stone, and also cement and supplies which came by the railroad. They had to cut a road from the main road through to the cove.

But one thing was not brought by the flivver, and that was the suction dredge, a horrible monster, a kind of jumble of house and machinery which came on a big six-ton truck and was launched into the lake. Its whole ramshackle bulk shook and shivered when it was in operation sucking the bottom of the lake up through a big pipe and shooting it through another long pipe which terminated on the land. Thus sand and gravel were secured and at the same time the lake was dredged by this mammoth vacuum cleaner. The pipeline which terminated on the shore was supported on several floats a few yards apart, and the first scout to perform the stunt of walking on this pulsating thing was — —

Guess.

About a week after work on the dam had begun, Tom rode over to the cove on the truck with Robin Hood. He had struck up a friendship with the stranger and liked him, as every one did. The young man was quiet, industrious, intelligent. He did not encourage questions about himself, but Tom was the last one to criticise reticence.

Moreover, labor was scarce and willing workers in demand. One thing which gave the young man favor in camp was his liking for the younger boys, who frequently rode back and forth with him.

"Well, it's beginning to look like a dam, isn't it?" Tom said, as they rode along. "You won't be able to get much more stone up behind the pavilion.... The dam ought to raise the lake level about five or six feet, the engineers say. That'll mean moving a couple of the cabins back. Storm was a good thing after all, huh?"

"I guess it will be remembered around these parts for a good many years," Tom's companion said.

"And you were out in the thick of it," said Tom, in his usual cheery way. "Up on the mountain it was terrible."

"On the mountain? I was—I was just in the woods. It was bad enough there."

He looked sideways at Tom, rather curiously. He liked Tom but he could never make up his mind about him. It always seemed to him, as indeed it seemed to others, that Tom's cheery, simple, offhand talk bespoke a knowledge of many things which he did not express. It was often hard to determine what he was really thinking about.

"I think I'll see that face whenever it storms," Tom said.

"What face?"

"Harlowe's; he was just staring up in the air. Ever see a person who has suffered violent death, Hood?"

"Once."

"Funny thing, did you ever hear how the eyes of a dead man reflect the last thing he saw? I know over in France they often saw images in the eyes of dead soldiers. Near Toul, where I was stationed, they carried in a dead Frenchy and you could see an airplane in his eyes just as sure as day."

"Did you—did you ever see anything like that?"

"Oh, sure. Ask any army surgeon or nurse."

Hood did not seem altogether satisfied with the answer. He was clearly perturbed. But he did not venture another question, and for a few minutes neither spoke.

"Another thing, too, speaking of France," said Tom. "We could always pick out a fellow that came over from England as soon as they set him to driving an ambulance. He'd always go plunk over to the left side of the road. You know they have to keep to the left over there instead of to the right——"

"Yes, I know——" Hood began, and stopped short.

"Been over there, eh?"

"I'm not English, but I lived there several years, and drove a car."

"Yes?" Tom laughed. "Well, now, I just noticed how you kept edging over to the left. I didn't think anything about your coming from England, but I just happened to notice it. Takes a long time to get a habit out of your nut, doesn't it? People might say you were reckless and all that when really it would just be that habit that you couldn't get away from. I've got so as I can tell a Pittsburgh scout, or a Canadian scout just from little things—little habits."

"You're a pretty keen observer," said Hood; "that about the eyes of a dead person interests me. When you made that discovery up on the mountain, do you mean——"

"Your engine isn't hitting on all four, Hood," Tom interrupted.

They both listened for a minute.

"Guess not," said the driver.

"Wire off, maybe," Tom suggested.

Hood stopped the machine and got out. It would have been more like Tom to jump out and investigate for himself, especially since he had run the old truck long before Hood had ever seen it. But he did not do it. Instead, he remained seated. Hood was right, there was nothing whatever the matter with the engine. He wondered how Tom could have thought there was.

Tom seemed not greatly interested until his companion climbed in, then he craned his neck out and looked down where Hood had been standing.

"All right," he finally said; "I was wrong, as usual."

"I think you're usually right," laughed Hood.

Whatever the cause, Tom seemed thoughtful and preoccupied for the rest of the journey. He whistled some, and that was a sign that he was thinking. Once he seemed on the point of saying something.

"Hood, do you — —" he began. Then fell to whistling again.

And so in a little while they came to the cove.

CHAPTER XXXIV
THE MESSAGE

The altogether thrilling and extraordinary occurrence which is all that remains to be told in this narrative, was witnessed by a dozen or more scouts. It happened, as deeds of heroic impulse always happen, suddenly, so that afterwards accounts differed as to just how the thing had occurred. There are always several versions of dramatic happenings. But on one point all were agreed. It was the most conspicuous instance of outright and supreme heroism that Temple Camp had ever witnessed or known. And because there was no scout award permissible in the occasion, the boys of camp, with fine inspiration, named the new dam after the hero, who with soul possessed challenged the most horrible monster of which the human mind can conceive, threw his life into the balance with an abandon nothing less than sublime, and found his reward in the very jaws of horrible and ghastly death.

And the dam was well named, too, for it represented strength superseding weakness. If you should ever visit Temple Camp you should end your inspection in time to row across the lake in the cool of the twilight, when the sun has gone down behind the mountain, and take a look at Robin Hood's Dam.

The scene was the usual morning scene. The slanting sifter was dropping its rain of dirt through the grating and sending the stones rolling down. The mixer was revolving. A hundred feet or so from the shore the clumsy old dredge was drawing up sand from the bottom of the lake, and the big pipeline running to shore was pulsating so that the floats supporting it rocked in the water. At the end of this pipeline was a big pile of wet sand from the lake. Men were carrying this sand off in wheelbarrows.

A few of the scouts were busy at their favorite pastime of walking along this shaking pipeline to the dredge from which they would dive, then swim to the nearest point on shore and proceed again as before. Hervey

Willetts had been the Christopher Columbus to discover this endless chain of pleasure and he had punctuated it with many incidental stunts.

It was not altogether easy to walk on the trembling wet piping, but those who did it were of course in bathing attire, and with bare feet it was not so hard, once one got the hang of it.

The sight of this merry procession proceeding on its endless round proved too much for one pair of eyes that watched wistfully from the shore. One after another the dripping scouts came scrambling up out of the water, proceeded to the shore end of the pipeline, walked cautiously along it, feet sideways, crossed the dredge, dived and presently appeared again. "Follow your leader" they were singing and it was funny to hear how they picked up the tune and got into time upon emerging.

This kind of thing was hard to resist. It is hard not to dance when the music is playing. There was an alluring fascination about it.

Suddenly, to the consternation of every one, there was Goliath in the procession, moving along the pipeline, keeping his foothold by frantic gesticulations with his arms. He was laughing all over his little face. He swayed, he bent, he almost fell, he got his balance, almost lost it, got along a few steps, and then down he went with a splash into the water.

This climax of his wild enterprise occurred in a gap of the procession. Some scouts had fallen out, others were clambering out the other side of the dredge. So it happened that the splash was the first thing to attract attention.

Goliath did not reappear and before any one had a chance to dive or knew just where to dive, something was apparent, which sent a shudder through Tom Slade, who was standing near the end of the pipeline. The pouring forth of the wet sand out of the pipe ceased, or rather lessened and the substance shot out in little jerks. Tom, ever quick to see the significance of a thing, knew this for what it was. It was an awful message from the bottom of the lake.

Something was clogging up the suction pipe there.

CHAPTER XXXV

THE HERO

This thing, as I said, all happened in a flash. There was shouting, there was running about....

"Stop the machinery!" some one yelled.

"Reverse your engine!"

Tom felt himself thrust aside, lost his balance and fell into the deposit of wet sand. The pouring out of this had ceased.

"Don't let him do that! He's crazy!" some one shrieked.

"Reverse the engine; he'll come up. Don't dive—you! You'll be chewed to pieces."

"Who dived?" said Tom, scrambling to his feet.

"The body will come up when the suction stops."

"Both bodies, you mean; that crazy fool dived."

"They won't come up if they're wedged in. Keep her going—reversed."

Everybody crowded to the shore and to the deck of the dredge. The pulsating of the big line had ceased. Men shouted to do this, to do that. Others contradicted. All eyes were upon the water. They crowded each other, watching, waiting....

Then a red spot appeared on the surface. It spread and grew lighter in color as it mingled with the water. The watchers held their breath—gasped. The tension was terrible.

Then (as I said, it all happened in a flash) a hand covered with blood reached up and tried to grasp the nearest float. It disappeared, but Tom Slade had seen it and, jumping to the float, he reached down.

"I've got him—keep back—you'll sink the float——"

"Don't let go."

It was not in the nature of Tom Slade to let go.

Presently a ghastly face with red stained hair streaming over it, appeared.

"Let me take him," said Tom.

But the man with bleeding, mangled shoulder would not give up what he held, as in a grip of iron, with his other arm.

And so Tom Slade dragged the wounded creature up onto the float and there he lay in a pool of blood, still clinging to his burden.

The little boy was safe. He opened his eyes and looked about. His face was smeared with mud, one of his shoes was gone, his foot seemed to be twisted. It was all too plain that he had been within the suction pipe, within the devouring jaws of that monster serpent, when his frantic rescuer had dragged him back. But he was safe.

His rescuer was utterly crazed. Yet he seemed to know Tom.

"Safe—alive— —" he muttered.

"Yes, he's safe; lie still. Get the doctor, some of you fellows—quick."

"Send, send—them away—all. You know—do you—I'm square—yes?"

"Surely," said Tom soothingly. "Lie still."

"He's alive?"

"Yes."

"Listen, come close. I'll tell you—now. I murdered a kid once—now—now I've—I've saved one— —"

"Shh. It's the same one, Harlowe."

"You—you know?"

"Yes, I know. We'll talk about it after. Hold your head still—quiet—that's right. Don't think about it now. Shh—I think your arm is broken; don't move it."

"I—I—killed— —"

"No, you never killed any one. Lie still—please. I know all about it. We can't talk about it now. But you never killed any one, remember that."

"You know I'm Harlowe?"

"Yes. Don't talk. That was little Willie Corbett you saved. Now don't ask me any more now; please. You don't think I'm a liar, do you? Well, I'm telling you you never killed anybody. See? You're not a murderer, you're a hero. I know all about it.... Lie still, that's right.... Don't move your arm...."

CHAPTER XXXVI

Harlowe's Story

Aaron Harlowe was lying on his cot in the little rustic hospital at Temple Camp. It was worth being sick to lie in that hospital. It was just a log cabin. The birds sang outside of it, you could hear the breeze blowing in the trees, you could hear the ripple of paddles on the lake.

Tom Slade sat upon the side of the cot.

"You see when I found the map, I knew you had gone up the mountain. And I didn't think you'd go up there unless there was some one up there that you knew. The light was up there before you went up. Now that you tell me you went up there to hide with that friend of yours, everything fits together. I knew there must have been two of you up there, because I saw your footprint. You have a patch on the sole of your shoe and the dead man didn't. See? When I asked you to get out of the auto it was just because I wanted to see your footprint. Your always getting over to the left hand side of the road made me a little suspicious. Footprints don't lie and that clinched it."

"But did you see my image in the eyes of the dead man?" Harlowe asked weakly.

"I saw an image of a man; I couldn't tell it was you. But I knew some one else had been there. Do you feel like telling me the rest now? Or would you rather wait."

"You seem to know it all," Harlowe smiled. It was pleasant to see that smile upon his pale, thin face.

"It isn't what you know, it's what you do that counts," said Tom softly. "And see what you did. Talk about heroism!"

It was from the desultory talk which followed that Tom was able to piece out the story, the mystery of which he had already penetrated. Harlowe, in fear of capture after his supposed killing of the child, had sought refuge in the hunting shack of his friend upon the mountain. There the two had lived till the night of the storm. When Harlowe's friend had been crushed under the tree, Harlowe had bent over him to make sure that he was dead. It was then, in the blinding storm, that his license cards had fallen out of his pocket and, by the merest chance, on the open coat of the dead man.

Harlowe said that after that he had intended to give himself up, but that when he read that Harlowe had been discovered, and no doubt buried, he had resolved to let his crime and all its consequences be buried with the dead man, who like himself was without relations.

But Harlowe's conscience had not been buried, and it was in a kind of mad attempt to square himself before Heaven, and still the voice of that silent, haunting accuser, that he had performed the most signal act of heroism and willing sacrifice ever known at Temple Camp.

As Tom Slade emerged after his daily call on the convalescent, a song greeted his ear and he became aware of Hervey Willetts, hat, stocking and all, coming around the edge of the cooking shack. He was caroling a verse of his favorite ballad:

"The life of a scout is kind,

is kind,

His handbook he never can find,

can find.

He don't bother to look,

In the little handbook.

The life of a scout is kind."

"Hunting for your handbook, Hervey?"

"I should fret out my young life about the handbook."

"Walking my way?"

"Any way, I'm not particular."

"Cross come yet?"

"I haven't seen it. Do you think it would look good on my hat?"

"Why, yes," Tom laughed. "Only be sure to pin it on upside down."

"Why?"

"Why, because then when you're standing on your head, it'll be right side up. See?"

"Good idea. I guess I will, hey?"

"Sure, I—I double dare you to," said Tom.

END